I0703046

# Winter Blossoms

Lisa Keifer

Copyright © 2023 by Lisa Keifer

First paperback edition: 2024

ISBN: 979-8-9906604-2-7

All rights reserved.

This is a work of fiction. Names, characters, places, and incidents are either the product of the author's imagination or used fictitiously. Any resemblance to actual persons, living or dead, events, or locales is entirely coincidental.

No portion of this book may be reproduced in any form without written permission from the copyright owner, except as permitted by U.S. copyright law and for the use of quotations in a book review. For more information, address: lisakeifer@lisakeiferauthor.com

Cover Design: Sarah Kil Design Studio

Editor: Joanne Lui, JL Editing Services

# Chapter 1

## Alec

I DON'T KNOW THE woman I'm looking for, but I hope with everything in me that it's her. I've never been here at Blooming Cascade Floral Design before—never been to Syracuse Falls at all, as far as I can recall—but my mom just got engaged, and my brother Henry's girlfriend, Effie, sent me here for the best flowers in the entire Syracuse region. I still don't see why I couldn't just order some from a florist in town, especially online, but Effie insisted I come here in person.

Frankly, flowers all look the same to me, though, so maybe I don't have the right eye. But this woman in front of me? Oh, she has it. I know she does.

She smiles. It's warm, welcoming, cheerful, and a little wise, to be honest. Like she knows exactly what I want before I even open my mouth. She has dark hair to her shoulders and greenish-blueish eyes that I wish I could lose myself in. The chill from being out in the bitter January cold snap is already leaving my body.

"Hi," she says, her voice just as bright as the expression she wears on her face. I've heard women say that one look from a man and they turn into puddles, which always sounded so stupid to me. I get it now.

I feel like I've stared at her too long, so I dart my eyes away, just for a second, as I reply, "Hi." Then my mind goes blank, and I can't think of anything else to say. Nothing. Not a single word.

She tries encouraging an answer out of me. "Can I help you find something?"

Then I remember. "I'm Alec. I'm looking for Lourdes."

"Oh, I'm sorry. She isn't here. I'm Marcy."

I hear Marcy's words, but I'm still so taken with her that I can't say what I want or need. "Flowers," I finally mumble. I feel like an idiot right now, completely unable to form coherent sentences. I grimace, but I also kind of grin when she smiles at me. I also really hope she doesn't think I'm as ridiculous as I'm acting right now.

"What would you like? Do you have any specific ones in mind?"

Again, my brain can't seem to force my mouth to say anything. The closest I get to speaking is licking my lips, which now I realize might give her the wrong impression. I'm several inches taller than her, silently standing here licking my lips. I bet I look like a freaking creeper. And then I make it worse with the only words that come to mind. "What do you offer?"

Damn it.

Marcy doesn't flinch, though, so maybe that's a good sign. "We have custom-designed as well as premade bouquets. We also have our DIY station over there." She motions to an area with a bunch of different flowers in long conical-looking buckets, placed on some sort of rack that makes them almost horizontal.

I look back at her without an answer. I don't have one to give since I didn't think buying flowers would be this complicated. I usually just stop at the place near me for girlfriends and dates, or kindly ask my assistant to send arrangements, if need be.

Marcy walks away from me, toward the end of the counter by an open inner door. Then she motions for me to follow her. We end up in front of the standing coolers that are kind of like refrigerators, but for flowers, with clear glass doors showcasing many color combinations of bouquets in clear vases.

I stay quiet as Marcy explains what kinds of flowers are in each of these, all available for purchase without much thought on my part, which is probably best right now. If I had to come up with a design at this moment, it would end up some sort of monstrosity that either the designers or Marcy would laugh at me for. Not something I'd like to happen.

"What are the big selling flowers right now?" I ask.

"Winter blossoms, the ones in season. Honestly, though, with the way we source our flowers and greenhouses, customers can pretty much get any flower any time they want."

"Any winter blossoms a favorite of yours?"

She's quiet for a moment. "I'm partial to the star magnolia, but it's often more in spring than winter, though in some places, it blooms in late February."

Her voice is so pretty, I think as she talks on. It's high-pitched but not squeaky. Almost angelic, if it isn't weird to think that about a woman I just met. Well, half-met. I haven't been able to tell her my name yet. All I can do right now is listen to that sweet voice explain things about these flowers that I love hearing and will still probably forget. The shine on her happy, animated face is beautiful, too. It's clear she loves working here. I also think maybe she has some sort of makeup or something on that's making her skin a little sparkly. Whatever it is, I love it.

"How about this one?" Marcy opens one of the cooler doors to our left and pulls out a bouquet with orange and red flowers, as well as some small yellow ones and a bit of greenery. She even sniffs it before offering it to me to smell. Whatever the scent of this, I need to bottle it and keep it. Or just have those flowers on hand with me everywhere, just so I can remember the look of joy on her face when breathing in its aroma.

"Is this your favorite arrangement?" I ask, suddenly able to find my voice.

Marcy nods. "They're sweet peas—that's the red ones—and chrysanthemums—the orange-yellow ones."

Sweet peas and chrysanthemums. And she's right. They smell great.

Marcy guides me back to the register at the counter. I pay, then she asks something about the flowers.

"Yes," I say automatically, not having heard her words.

When her happy expression falters then drops completely, I think back on what she said. Then it hits me. She asked if these are for my girlfriend. One I don't have. But I was stupidly fawning over that beautiful voice again and not listening to what Marcy was saying, which is never good.

"Actually—"

The door opens, and a loud group of women enter the shop, bringing with them a burst of cold air. Marcy immediately says bye to me and turns to the new group with greetings and questions of how she can help them. I'm gently crowded out of where I'm standing by the women, who clearly have a lot of questions to ask Marcy. But I can't leave. Not when she thinks I lusted after her, then bought flowers for a girlfriend.

I hang back, out of the way, my hands in my wool coat pockets. There's a wall full of vases on shelves, so I walk over to that area and look at each one, glancing back to Marcy every other second to see if she's free yet. She isn't. In fact, she doesn't take any time to stop and look over at me.

She takes an order from someone on the phone, then another from a man who comes in with a woman who appears to be his wife. Then Marcy spends an inordinate amount of time showing the first group the DIY flower station. Apparently, these ladies are from out of town, and while they were hanging out in the vintage market nearby, someone mentioned that they should come check out this place. All this time, Marcy still hasn't looked at me. At first, maybe it was safe for her to assume I left, but we are closer now. She knows I'm here.

Because I don't want to be creepy and hover nearby, I step away from them toward a corner in the front. Based on the clock on the wall behind the register, it's been eight minutes since I paid for the flowers I still hold in my right hand. Eight minutes second-guessing how interested she might be when I get to tell her the truth.

Finally, every other customer has left, and it's just Marcy and me.

She goes to the counter again and clicks a few things on her computer.

I hurry over to her, unconcerned with how desperate I look right now. Except I can't speak again. At least she's looking at me now. While she doesn't seem surprised, she does appear curious.

"No girlfriend," I manage to spit out.

"Sorry?" she asks.

I shake my head and clear my throat, trying to steady myself. "I don't have a girlfriend. These are for my mom. I just . . . I got nervous. You make me nervous. In a good way," I add with a wide grin.

Marcy's scrunched face relaxes and lights up. Finally, she gives me the thing I've waited ten minutes to see again. She smiles.

# Chapter 2

## Marcy

"I'M SO GLAD TO hear you say that," I gush with a relieved sigh. I can't help myself. Men don't typically fluster me, even those as sexy and yet adorable as Alec, and it is so good to know he isn't the man I just assumed he was. "I've been fuming at you for the past ten minutes, thinking you flirted with me when you had a girlfriend. I didn't like that."

Alec dips his head a little but maintains eye contact. "Neither do I." Then he clams up again. He opens his mouth once, and I can see it has a bit of a tremble. No words squeak out. His cheeks flush. His gorgeous emerald-green eyes would probably blush if they could.

I really do make him nervous after all. "How do you feel about women asking men out?"

He lets a breath out that, to me, seems like it comes from a place of relief. "So long as the date happens, who cares who asks? Who cares who proposes, for that matter, so long as they both want it." Then his eyes pop open like he totally didn't mean for that last sentence to slip out. "Sorry. I just . . . These flowers are for my mom. She just got engaged. Not like I'm thinking of us getting engaged. It's too soon. I—" He stops and scrubs his left hand over his face.

I hold in a chuckle at how adorable he is. I don't care if he's this nervous around all women he's interested in. It's freaking sexy, and I love it.

"Let me guess," I say, giving him a chance to breathe. "Your mom proposed to her fiancé?"

Alec smiles. "She did. They were at his cabin out on Onondaga Lake. Mom said they were sitting in front of the warm fireplace, and it felt like the perfect time."

"I guess when you know, you know."

The way Alec looks at me puts a heat into my cheeks. *No, cheeks,* I silently scold them. *We are* not *doing that right now.* They could at least wait until Alec leaves. And I mean . . . *when you know, you know?* Oh my. Those words with that face—I swear I think I'm a goner right now. I have never, ever believed in love at first sight. Not for real life. But this man is certainly challenging that, whether he realizes it or not.

Based on the way his eyes take in my eyes and face, I can tell he might be inclined to believe in insta-love as well. Or at least *major* insta-attraction and connection.

When he opens his mouth, I'm certain he's going to ask me out. He just has that air about him. Or maybe I'm expecting it because it's the next natural step. We are attracted. We clicked. Neither of us is attached. Let's date!

"Well, thanks for the flowers." He stumbles over his words.

And . . .

Then he doesn't say anything else. At all.

That's it?

I don't get more?

There wasn't a date invitation in there anywhere. It was a complete shutdown and shutout.

"Oh," I say softly. I can feel my facial expression slink down into blankness. "Okay. Hope your mom likes them."

Alec silently stares at me again. He doesn't even bother stuttering anything to give me an idea of what he's thinking.

"Well, thanks," he says again. Then he gives me a stupid "see ya" kind of wave and he's out the door, leaving me victim to another icy blast of air.

# Chapter 3

Alec

Stupid man.

I am a stupid, *stupid* man.

Marcy was watching me with hearts in her eyes, and I just acted like none of the flirting happened between us before walking out. I didn't even ask her on a date or ask if I could kiss her—which, with as much as I already like her, isn't out the realm of possibility of things I might say. Nope. I just walked my dumb ass out the door without so much as a look back at her.

She must hate me already. Or at least recoil at the idea of me now.

I unlock my car, put my left hand on the frigid handle, then stare at the flowers Marcy picked out that are still in my right. After a chuckle, I let go of the handle, lock the car again, and carefully jog back into the flower shop, mindful of the snowy and icy spots on the pavement and sidewalk. Marcy looks up at me, eyes wide, a scowl on her face, yet a laugh in her throat.

"Back so soon?"

"I'm not seeing her today. My mom. I think I need to order flowers to send to her."

Marcy eyes the bouquet I bought. "Are you planning on returning that?"

"No," I answer quickly. "Of course not."

She looks relieved, but not enough. Her eyes are narrow. She bites her lips, but I think it's much less a "trying not to kiss me" thing and more a "trying not to insult me after my exit" thing.

"Sorry. I'm sorry. Not returning it. I just . . . didn't think," I stutter. "Didn't mean to leave like that."

"You came back," she replies. Does she think this is a good thing or a bad thing?

"I did. Sorry."

Now her brows crinkle toward each other. "You're sorry you came back."

I scrub my free hand over my face a few times. "No. Not at all." Then I remove my hand and look over at her, hoping she can read the context from my face since I might not be able to get the right words out. "I'm sorry I left without asking you out."

Her cheeks pink up again. I already love that color. I wonder if there's a flower around here that same shade. I'd buy a bouquet of them every day.

"Me too," Marcy finally says.

"I'd like to make up for that, if I may."

She laughs at the formality. I have to fight back a chuckle myself. This is officially the most awkward I have ever been with a woman.

Then Marcy gives me one of her beautiful grins. "I'd like that, too."

I smile at her, glancing at the flowers I forgot were still in my hand, then back up to my beautiful companion. "Would you be okay if I gave these to my assistant?"

Her face twists into confusion, and I know I just screwed up. Again.

# Chapter 4

## Marcy

Alec wants to give the flowers I specifically chose—just so I could tell him they were my favorites—to someone else? I take back what I said before about not caring how awkward he is with other women. But I have to know . . .

"Does she make you as nervous as I do?"

He immediately shakes his head, his short, light brown hair reflecting a bit of light in the process. "Not even a little bit."

I can't hold in the smile that bubbles up. "Then I don't mind. That's really sweet of you, by the way. Giving flowers to your assistant instead of making her order them."

"She's a good person." Alec says this with a kind voice, and thankfully does not give off any hint of having wanted her at some point.

We put together a custom order for his mom's floral arrangement. I figured he would have picked one of our regular sellers, but then, he doesn't seem like he wants to leave. A custom order definitely takes longer. I am not complaining one bit.

Alec doesn't know his mom's favorite flowers, but he does know that she likes red and pink.

"Here," I say as I click on a photo of an arrangement we've done in the past. "We can add in some orange tones, so it looks balanced and not like it's for Valentine's Day."

He nods at the picture. "I like that. It looks happy, I guess."

"It's the bright colors," I reply. "And the daisies. Daisies make everything happy. We can also add in some leucadendron for a bit of height and something a little different. Lourdes put an order in for the leucadendron not long ago, so it should be here before your mom's arrangement needs finished."

"Sounds good."

I look up at Alec. His attention is on me. It's been so long since I had these fluttery feelings from a man looking at me like that. I want to reach up and caress his cheek, but that might be too much. It would *definitely* be too much to lean up and kiss that cheek, but this knowledge doesn't stop my brain—or maybe my heart—from insisting that I should do it anyway. I refrain.

"Since you don't have any more specifics that you need, whoever designs it can fill in the rest of the blanks in terms of how it looks based on budget and what's available."

Alec nods. "Can I make it a pick up instead of delivery?"

I'm a little surprised at this, but more than that, I'm ecstatic. My whole body is so warm now, I need to fan myself. "You don't have to do that just to see me again."

His face flushes. I bet he's as warm as I am. If I stepped around this stupid counter between us, I'd be able to feel it. But doing so would mean being farther away from him, and I don't like that idea, even though it would only be temporary.

"How did you know?" he asks.

"For one thing, we did just admit to wanting a date."

He laughs. "Right. Sorry."

We decide on delivery to his mom's house for the floral arrangement.

"About that other thing . . ." Alec begins.

"I close up in about twenty minutes," I say, glancing at the computer to be sure.

"Do you close at six every day?"

I mean, he could just look at the door or at our website later for an answer, but I know why he's asking, and I love it. "Only on weekdays. Weekends are eight to noon. I don't usually work weekends, though. Only when necessary."

"Hungry?" That sweet, awkward smile he was wearing has turned into a sweet, slightly more confident one, and I love that, too.

I lock the back door, the last job I have to do at the end of the day. Knowing Alec stands behind me waiting to take me to dinner—our first date—has my skin covered in goosebumps. He insists on driving me, even though we are only headed a few blocks away. After his third mention of not wanting me to get cold, I knew I wasn't going to win the "walk or drive" debate, and wanted to kiss him for it.

The moment I turn to face him, Alec takes my left hand in his. If holding his hand is this spine-tingling in the very best way, I can't wait for the rest. He's not even nervous anymore. Actually, Alec seems to have transformed into a suave, super confident man, and I am here for it. I guess me accepting his date invite melted his insecurities. I like him any and every way, but the way he tenderly commands my attention is simply the best.

He uses his other hand on the small of my back to smoothly guide me to his car—which he remote-started so we could be warm as soon as we were seated. I had a feeling this city boy might be a little shocked at the Falls only offering two restaurant choices, but Alec never flinched or faltered. He jumped at the chance to stay in town for our meal, though I was more than willing to head into Syracuse. Still am, honestly. While I love Capelli's, it is nice to try new places.

Above all, though, I'm far too excited to have this date with Alec to care where we go or what we do. Gas station hot dogs? Absolutely. Can of beans cooked in a fire pit? You bet. Burnt and blackened to a crisp, completely unrecognizable grilled cheese sandwiches? Let's do it. At least at Capelli's, the food is guaranteed to be not only edible but delicious. What's also delicious? That way Alec looks at me as we slowly take step after step, as if he can't believe this is actually happening. Same, Alec, I think. I can't believe I'm lucky enough to have him here with me. Although we just met, it feels like this date is long overdue.

We make it to his car in no time at all and are quickly enveloped in glorious heat as soon as the doors are shut.

"You ready for this?" he asks.

I think the heat in my cheeks is now warmer than anything that's coming out of his car's vents. "More than."

We had to let go of each other to get in the car in our separate doors, but Alec quickly takes my hand. The car is still in park. Even though he's buckled in, he turns his whole body toward me. "I want you to know that it's been years since I've wanted to go on a date with a woman as much as I want to date you."

I'm so surprised that I don't immediately have a reply.

Alec speaks before I find my voice. "Tell me something you want me to know before we head out."

"What do you mean?" I can't hide the fact that he caught me off guard.

"Restaurants, while excellent places to subdue hunger, are not always conducive to intimate conversation."

I take a few moments before replying. I want this to mean as much as he's hoping it will. No wasting it on my favorite color. "In all my years of working at the flower shop, not once have I seen a man care so much about what kind of flowers he bought his mom or what they looked like. You already had my attention, but you earned my respect in those moments." And second by second—with every kind look and touch and word—you add to my growing affection for you.

He gives my hand a quick squeeze and leans closer to me. I'm almost afraid he's going to try for our first kiss so soon, but instead, he gently lifts my hand to his mouth, carefully curling his hand so mine is nearer to him before pressing his lips to my skin just below my knuckles.

"Anything else?" Alec's mouth is still close enough to brush against me as he speaks, his breath caressing my skin along my hand and down my wrist.

I move my eyes to see the spot that I wish could hold onto this feeling forever before catching his gaze once more. "I'm all in with this date. Wherever it leads us," I add as a quick afterthought, afraid he might be scared off by my enthusiasm.

His lips softly make contact with my skin again. "I'm all in for all of this, too."

There is no calming my giddy reaction, my pounding heart, or my shallow breathing. "Also, I hate capers, even though the chicken parm I order is practically smothered in them."

He laughs, lowering our hands down to the center console. "Dare I ask why?"

"I would drink nothing but caper smoothies the rest of my life if I was allowed to also eat their chicken parm."

Alec gives me a glowing smile. "Order the chicken parm from Capelli's. Good to know."

"That can't possibly be true," Alec says, shifting to the side in an apparent attempt to touch my arm with his. We are tucked into a corner table at Capelli's, a local restaurant in Syracuse Falls. Instead of sitting across from me, Alec chose the seat next to me, meaning we are at an angle to each other. He practically falls out of his chair from the movement to reach me.

I have to work hard to stifle my laughter enough to be able to reply. But I also slide my chair along the carpeted floor in Alec's direction, giving him better access to me. "I swear. If I hadn't seen it with my own eyes . . ."

"Every single flower you offer all together in one vase?"

I nod. "One and only one of each."

"How many was that?" He thinks a moment, then pretty much answers his own question. "It's got to be, what, at least several dozen? More?"

"I lost count. It was crazy. Lourdes even went so far as to slice the stems in half and cut off blooms just to make them all fit. And the vase was more like a bucket or barrel. But the customer was very specific, and very wealthy. Lourdes was too tempted by the ridiculousness of it to say no."

"Will I find a photo of it on your website?"

Now I let my laugh out with gusto. "Oh no. You'd think it would have looked like a meadow in a vase or something, but it didn't. It was hideous. Lourdes would fire me if I made pictures of it public."

"We definitely can't have that happen," Alec tells me. He's finally scooted his chair close enough to me—though not as casually as he attempted to make it seem. Except our arms are at a weird angle to each other. Giving up on the pretense of playing it cool, Alec reaches over and takes my hand. We've already finished our food and have just ordered homemade chocolate cake for dessert.

"What's your funny story?" I ask at the same time he says, "What other crazy orders have you received?"

We smile at each other.

I've talked about myself all night. My likes and interests. Family and friends. Childhood and teen years. We've actually been here for over to hours, much to the chagrin of the waitstaff. But Alec has been buying coffee and dessert just to keep our table. He doesn't seem like he's in the mood to share his own stories.

"Please," he says, bringing me back to our current conversation. He wants to know more crazy orders? Does he have any idea how many things can go wrong in a flower shop? Gazing into his gorgeous, deep-green eyes, I can't help but give him what he asks for. If he looks at me like that much longer, I might be inclined to give him more. So much more. Probably not a good idea.

I haven't given *more* in years. I've never slept with a guy before the tenth date, except for one: Dipshit Dane, my ex, who dumped me two years ago. Dane got *everything* on the first date. No one else has reached that special milestone with me since him.

*Dumped*. If that isn't the best description of it, I can't possibly think of a better one.

Wait.

I take that back. Yes, I can think of a better word: *Abandoned*. Dane abandoned me.

Before that moment—the moment my heart shattered and my walls went up, Dane was the perfect, flawless star athlete, the kind of guy all the ladies love. Compare that to me, the woman who hates sunlight unless it's through a window and who also relishes in any activity that doesn't require me to use a ball or mitt or racket or net of any kind.

While I didn't lie to myself and think what Dane and I had was love, I thought it was at least something precious. Something that could—*would*—turn into love one day. Joke was on me, I guess. I will never understand what he saw in me or why he insisted our differences didn't matter. Because they did.

This was made crystal clear five months into our relationship when he practically kicked me out of his car because his friend suddenly came up with Final Four tickets and they had to pack and book a flight. This apparently meant he had to leave immediately in order to get to the game on time, even though it wasn't until the next day. I was left standing on the sidewalk, calling friends for a ride home to the Falls from Camillus, despising the fact that there was no rideshare car available to me. That was the end of Dane for me. That's when he earned his nickname.

People can say opposites attract all they want, but all that tells me is that their lust was too strong to want to deal with reality. I should have known better with Dipshit Dane. I hope to know Alec better before completely falling for his charms, which already have a hold on me. The worst part is, they come naturally, I think. Dane was always putting up a front, always trying to be Mr. Smooth. Alec tries, but he's not ashamed that he's so nervous around me, too. It's the perfect combination.

We leave the restaurant in Syracuse, then he asks if I feel like walking around downtown. I give a little laugh. "It's a bit too chilly for that."

He looks down at our clothes, realizing that I'm still in my work flats and not boots. "Guess we aren't as bundled as we should be."

I shake my head. "Sadly, no." Then I spy a tiny park just down the way with a bench in it. I motion in that direction. "We can spend a few more minutes out here, if you'd like."

Alec's already reaching to silently ask for my hand. "I'd like."

Hands clasped, we walk to the corner, cross the street, and make it to the bench, where he sits down so close to me, our respective body heat immediately mingles. We had no reason to worry about being cold because the heat coming off of Alec could melt entire glaciers. I don't even notice the temperature around us anymore. January? Ha. Feels more like July to me.

Alec turns to look at me. I wait for him to speak. A slow smile pulls at the right side of his mouth. "How do you feel about surprises?"

"Love them," I say, giving a grin of my own.

Now his grows to spread across his face. "What day are you off next week?"

"I'm scheduled Sunday and then Saturday next week since we have a lot of winter weddings this year, so I have Monday off. Why?" I tilt my head, letting him know I'm intrigued by his questions.

"What would you say if I told you I have a surprise in mind for you? A date for us. Too soon? Too presumptuous?"

He watches me, waiting for an answer. Suddenly, he's Nervous Alec from the flower shop again. It's so damn sexy. "Not too soon," I say, my voice a murmur as Alec scoots closer and turns my body so my legs cross over his. He then tentatively places his hands on my hips. There is no space left between us, and I am so here for that. "Not soon enough."

Alec chuckles, and honestly, it's yet another sexy thing he does. There isn't an action I've seen of him that I'm not attracted to. "We can't plow through all the dates I have in mind in one day. We need things to look forward to."

I look forward to seeing a *lot* of him, but I don't say this. Instead, I smile, then lean up and give him the lightest kiss on the jaw. "I don't kiss on the first date, so that's another thing we have to look forward to."

A half groan-half moan tumbles out of him, and he pulls me closer. He's positioned me so my legs are over him, but I shift where I'm now straddling him. Alec makes that grumbly sound again and buries his face into my neck. "I'm looking forward to as many kisses with you as I can get, whether that happens tonight or tomorrow or two months from now."

"Definitely won't have to wait two months," I whisper. I'm not sure I can wait another two minutes.

Yet I need to.

My rules for dating exist for a reason. Alec and I haven't spent enough time together to move to the next stage.

Except my legs are wrapped around his waist, and I can feel exactly how much he likes that. With all of *that*, it still isn't as much as I like it.

"We should probably go," I reluctantly say. "I'm sure there's nothing like getting frostbite on a first date. Makes it memorable in the wrong way."

He laughs, drops a kiss on my neck his face is still buried in, then pulls back to give me a grin. "That is absolutely not the way I want this date to go."

After he drives me to my car, which is still at Blooming Cascade, I leave the flower shop and head to my apartment in the Apple Lane complex. I've lived on the third floor in one of the four three-story buildings for a few years now. Before that, I rented an apartment over in Camillus, which was where I met Dane. I love the small-town feel of Syracuse Falls, though. It's the cutest little village surrounded by a developing metropolis, or at least it seems that way to me.

Once I've settled onto my favorite plush, cocoon-like chair, I reach next to me and pick up the brand-new Jane Austen-themed quote-a-day journal I bought a few weeks ago and haven't done anything with yet. It has a gorgeous sapphire-blue hardcover with embossed lettering, gold gilt-edged pages, and lines for five years of entries for each day. I open the book to today's date and read its quote: *It is not time or opportunity that is to determine intimacy; it is disposition alone. Seven years would be insufficient to make some people acquainted with each other, and seven days are more than enough for others.*

Then I lean over again, grab my basic blue ink pen, and write my first entry.

*Had a date tonight. First in months. Alec. He's awkward and sexy and kind, and I want more of him than I'll probably get. Been too long since I caught the eye of a good man.*

I pause my hand, then I add:

*If I do get more of him, what happens if—or when—I have to let him go?*

# Chapter 5

## Marcy

IT'S BEEN TWO DAYS since I saw Alec. I almost feel absurd missing him this much already. We just met. I can't possibly be head over heels like this so soon. It's a *good* thing he had plans last night, made before he knew me. Not something I need to feel sad about. *Hear that, brain?*

Work was long today. All of it. I ran the front counter in addition to mocking up and scheduling the next five social media posts for the shop. On top of that, I've been helping organize all the online Valentine's Day orders. Even though it's three and a half weeks away, people want their orders in before they assume supplies for certain bouquets and arrangements run out, even though we are as well-stocked as we can be.

So even though I was supposed to be done at noon, I'm just arriving home at three. My date with Alec tonight isn't until six, which gives me plenty of time to relax and refresh, including taking another shower and redoing my hair and makeup.

First things first, though. I whip up some instant hot cocoa mix—the only kind of cocoa I ever drink—with warm cream and sit in my favorite cocoon chair, my new journal in hand. I left my pen in between the pages last night after my newest entry. The Austen quote of the day? *It is well to have as many holds upon happiness as possible.*

It feels like the right time for today's.

*Have another date with Alec tonight. Can't wait.*

Here I draw a little happy face with heart eyes and hearts nearby. There are so many other words and phrases spinning around in my head, like *miss* and *adore* and *kiss*, and it's too soon for all of them. In an effort to take my time and sort them out, I spend a few seconds flipping through the pages of the book from the back to the front. But, wait . . . why is there different colored ink on that page?

There's . . . *writing* in this journal? Someone else owned this journal before I did?

That doesn't make any sense to me since it was in a bookstore that only sells new books. I mean, it wasn't sealed in some sort of plastic packaging when I bought it, but it was still new. Only it wasn't. At least a quarter of November's pages as well as several of October's pages have been written on.

I don't know what to do with this information. I looked at the journal before purchasing it, flipping through to read some of the quotes. Somehow, I guess I didn't look close enough. My eyes return to the page with some stranger's handwriting on it.

*Wick called from school tonight, knowing we leave for a week in North Carolina tomorrow. He's hunkered down cramming for an exam he has coming up. Of course, he's studying far too early, but that is my Wick.*

Who is Wick? I check the date marked in the entries written by the unknown person. Eight years ago? Wow. How long has this journal been sitting on the shelf of the bookstore, holding on to a secret like this? And who would return a used journal? Or why? No one else looked at it? Maybe no one cared. Did someone write in it while sitting at the cafe or something as a joke? What happened?

Honestly, if I hadn't written my own three entries, I would take it back and get a refund. Would anyone believe me, though? That the other writing isn't mine?

I flip through the pages again, one by one this time. No one wrote their name in the front pages, but maybe there is something that identifies them in some other way. Of course, if I do find an identifying name, then I have to figure out what to do. I mean, how can I give this back when I wrote in it, too? And maybe it got returned or left at the store for an important reason that I'm not privy to. My fingers slip faster over the blank pages. It's barely used, but there's just enough filled-in pages that slow me down. Honestly, they make me stop and focus.

*NN said he'd be home for Thanksgiving this year, which makes this mom's heart happy. Wick should be, but he's flying off to some computer convention or other in Seattle the weekend before (I try but never understand! And he never teases me, which also makes this mom's heart happy) He's afraid he might be too tired. I told him to come home anyway and sleep the whole weekend if need be. The holiday just wouldn't be the same without him here.*

In all the entries I find, there are only a handful of names: NN, Wick, Juliana (who seems to be this woman's friend), and the Turners and the Cosgroves, only mentioned by their last names. I don't even know where they are from so I can't exactly look them up. Could be Syracuse, where I got the book. Could be anywhere not in North Carolina.

Perusing her words again, I get the feeling this woman is married, what with all the uses of "we" instead of "I," yet she never mentions a spouse or significant other by name. I've only written three entries into this journal, and all three contain Alec's name. Not sure what this means.

My alarm sounds. The "absolutely have to start getting ready by this point or I'll be answering the door with a towel around my hair and no makeup on my face" one, which I set early this morning when I had an idea that I'd be stuck at the shop longer than usual.

As I apply the last of my lipstick, I hear a new text come in. It's Alec.

Alec: I have dinner scheduled to arrive soon, and popcorn is at the ready. Can't wait to see you.

He added a winking face, which simultaneously makes me blush and laugh. Initially, Alec had asked if I wanted to go ice skating, but I am so far from being an outdoor person that it isn't even funny. I don't do outside *anything*. I don't even visit Quill Bridge by the actual Syracuse Falls waterfall, which is the most shocking thing to every other resident in this tiny town. It's almost a rite of passage here to visit the falls.

I text him back that I can't wait to see him, either, and that I'm on my way. It doesn't take me long to find his place. He's very good at giving descriptions. And he's so cute when he blushes at being told so.

"Couldn't have you getting lost," he tells me with a barely there shrug, the pink still in his cheeks. There's also a sparkle in his eyes.

Alec and I didn't kiss on our first date. It's usually the second date that makes or breaks a kiss for me. If the date goes well, a liplock is a no-brainer. If it doesn't? No smooches for him. There haven't really been any in-betweens. Alec didn't push for a kiss on Thursday, but it's clear he'd very much like one tonight. I have to say I agree with him. Honestly, I was pretty dang close to breaking my "waiting until the second date" rule for him—a first since Dipshit Dane.

But here with Alec right in front of me, I don't want to wait until the end. I don't want this date to be over in order to feel what it's like to have his lips on mine. We are still in his foyer, the door an inch or so behind me, Alec an inch or so in front of me. His eyes have been glued to my face since I walked in. He watches my eyes before sliding his gaze down to my lips, up and over to my cheek, perhaps witnessing the glow of pink developing there, then up to my eyes once more.

"I'm glad you're here," he tells me, his breath hot on my skin. He smells like caramel. I can't wait to find out if he tastes like caramel, too.

"You said that already," I whisper with a smile. If I lean another half an inch, Alec would be on my mouth. I lean maybe a tenth of an inch closer. It's the slightest movement, barely noticeable, but just enough to sharpen the urge I have to kiss him right this moment.

He nods. My hands are at his neck, but with the warmth of him radiating into me, adding to my desire, I slide my fingers up in his hair and pull the rest of his body into a more convenient spot, leaving a gap barely wider than a pencil. I haven't told him my second-date rule, only that I don't kiss on first dates, but to hell with the rules anyway. I can't believe I didn't go beyond this with him on Thursday.

After another second, we've finally leaned near enough for our lips to just graze, the shock on my skin sending a message to my brain that we *need* more of that right now. I press in closer, pinning my mouth against his, pinning my whole body against him. There is an alluring, low-pitched moan, but I can't tell if it's coming from me or Alec. I'm far too swept up in how his lips move with mine, over mine, into mine. With every caress and nudge, every give and take, I want more. Running my hands over Alec's firm biceps and wide shoulders isn't enough. I have to feel him under this super-soft flannel shirt. I have to have our skin connecting in as many ways and places as possible.

I slowly—achingly slowly—slide my fingertips toward the bottom hem of his flannel shirt, from the tops of his muscled shoulders, along his collarbones, down his sternum, over his well-defined abs, and—finally—under the shirt onto his stomach, nothing in between my hand and Alec's body.

The moaning is definitely both of us this time.

And there's a knock at the door.

Alec pulls back, but not right away and not too far. I savor these extra seconds with him, wishing we didn't need to stop.

When he's about an inch away, he whispers, "Dinner's here."

"Yeah." But we don't move.

The delivery person knocks again, harder and faster this time. "I can't piss them off. I order from them a lot," he tells me.

I force myself to release my hands from him and step back so he can get the food. Alec gives the driver an apology and a tip, then we are thankfully alone again.

"Hungry?" Alec asks, returning to me, food bags in hand.

*Hungry for you*, I want to tell him, but much like the "no kissing until the end of the second date" rule, I also have a rule for how soon I can have sex with someone. This one isn't as easily brushed aside as the kissing one. When I broke it with Dipshit Dane, it was kind of reluctantly but with my full consent. That man earned my name for him long before we ever broke up. Long before it occurred to me to think of him that way. Thinking of him now clouds my mind, tamping down the smile I'd been giving Alec.

"Sure. Let's eat." I attempt to upturn my mouth again, but it's no use. I'm frustrated remembering how miserable I was back then, and Dipshit Dane strikes again.

I don't want to leave this apartment. That's what I've decided. I would happily spend my days and nights here with Alec and his gorgeous but grumpy orange tabby cat if I could. It's a great place, to be sure, but the main draw for me is the man sitting next to me on his sofa as we dine on Greek food. I've been talking about myself way too much again, per Alec's request, but I really need to put a stop to that. Just a few moments ago, I admitted to myself that I wouldn't mind living with Alec. Living with him. After only *two* dates. I'm a goner for sure, and I don't even know that much about him.

"You can't possibly want to hear any more about me," I finally say with a laugh.

Alec cocks his head and licks his lips. His gaze is on my mouth, just for a moment, then he looks me in the eye again. "I want to know everything about you."

I lean toward him enough to be able to nudge him with my shoulder. "And I feel the same about you."

He chuckles. "I can't imagine that my life is all that interesting."

"Okay, so start with something you do find interesting."

"I'm a little disappointed I don't get to see you in ice skates."

I give a soft laugh, then realize he's not joking. He'd asked if I wanted to go, but I never assumed he meant it. I'd replied with, *Right, because that's what I want to do on my Saturday . . .* "Wait. You were serious about the ice skating?"

I can't read the expression on his face as he replies. "Yes. Why else would I have asked you?"

It's a good question. Something I should have considered hours ago. "So you like skating?"

"Yes," he answers patiently.

"And other outdoor things." I assume so. My racing heart tells me I'm probably right. I speak before he can answer. My words are short and quick. "And sports? Does ice skating for you often mean hockey?"

"Typically, yeah." Alec's face is smiling, but my head is spinning.

"So, our ice skating could have been hockey instead?"

"If you were up for it, yeah. I don't know if you've ever played before, but I played all four years of high school and have been in adult leagues off and on since then. I could show you a few moves."

I ignore the flirty tone at the end. I am a stupid woman.

Forget Dipshit Dane. I'm Dipshit Marcy.

"You like hockey?" I sound like I'm being strangled.

Alec's smile fades. Mine has been gone ever since *hockey* forced itself into our conversation.

"I do. It's who Crunch is named after. I thought you realized that. Are you okay?" he asks.

He's too sweet to not have noticed that I can hardly breathe. I blink a million times a second, trying to force my brain to think something other than *run*. Except that's exactly what I need to do. I can't stay here. I can't be with Alec. He is the most perfect man apart from the one teeny, tiny, *giant* detail I scold myself for having not sussed out before now.

I put down—well, practically drop—my fork and rub my forehead roughly. Was it always this warm in here? Was the floor shaky when I got here? I can't stay. I can't dream of living in this amazing apartment with this incredible man day and night. This man is going to stomp all over my freaking heart.

In a short, hasty move, I abruptly stand, accidentally knocking my nearly empty plate off the coffee table in the process. "Sorry. I'm sorry." Alec and I both reach for the plate and fork. We grab the fork at the same time. His skin on mine again startles me so much, I involuntarily jump, dropping the utensil and backing away. "I have to go. I need to go home. Thanks." Then I grab my coat and purse and nearly sprint for the door.

The plate and fork clatter somewhere behind me, but I don't turn around to look. Then Alec is at my side again. "Please don't go. What happened? Are you sick? You shouldn't be driving if you feel ill. You can stay here."

I vigorously shake my head at that idea but can't seem to speak.

Alec's eyes are so damn kind as he watches me. "At least let me take you home."

"No," I reply immediately. Thank goodness my voice comes back when I need it. Too bad it's muted and wobbly. "I can't. You can't. Do that, I mean. No," I say again, in a firmer tone.

It takes less than a second for his face to scrunch all the way. "Can you please explain it to me? I don't understand. I don't get what's happening here. I thought we were having a good time. Things have been great with us. We have a date next week."

"We were. It was. We did. But now . . . I can't."

Alec reluctantly steps aside as I jerk the door open, not even bothering to put on my coat. My full hands restrict my ability to wipe away the hot tears trickling from my eyes as I sprint to my car.

"Marcy," Alec calls after me. I brave a glance back and see that he is on the sidewalk in only his socks. He didn't bother with a coat or jacket either, though he did shut the door so Crunch doesn't get out. "Please, tell me what's wrong." He's following after me. I can't let him do that. I can't let him in to my heart. I'll never survive it. I'll never survive him. And I sure as hell can't tell him why without drowning in the pain inflicted by Dane all over again as the perfect guy slips out of reach, metaphorically. Physically, he's right at my elbow, gently encouraging me to look at him.

"There's no other end for this," I tell him, my voice croaking. "There's no other path. This is it. I. Have. To. Go."

Alec gives me a look that says he doesn't want me to, yet he stands back anyway, enough for me to finally open my driver's side door.

I cry the whole way home. It's dark and the roads are a bit icy and I miss Alec already, down to my very core. I've never known a man as incredible as him.

Dipshit Marcy indeed.

# Chapter 6

## Alec

"Hello, sweetheart," Mom calls to me as I let myself into her house and quickly shut the door behind me, hoping to keep out the cold as much as possible.

It's been just over twelve hours since I saw Marcy. Ten hours since I last talked to her. Not even talked to her. I texted her long after she left my house, asking the same thing I asked before she was gone.

Me: Can you please explain it to me? I don't understand.

Marcy: It won't work. Trust me.

Trust her? Is she crazy? How can things have gone so well on our first date as well as our second, and then she hits me with a vague "it won't work," and I'm supposed to trust that? What about the connection we clearly have?

"Wick?" my mom says, much closer this time. She's using the nickname I've had since I can remember. I guess the L in Alec was too hard for my brother Henry to pronounce when he first met me, the day I was born.

I look over and find her only a few feet from me. I still haven't removed my coat or shoes. I'm stupidly standing on the rug next to the door, staring off into space, daydreaming about the woman who apparently wants nothing to do with me. "Hey, Mom." I lean over and kiss her cheek before she envelopes me in a quick hug.

"En-en is in the kitchen with Hudson," Mom adds.

Henry wasn't the only one who couldn't pronounce his brother's name. We all called him En-en, shortening it to NN in writing. Of course, once Henry and I hit our teen years, we reverted back to our regular names. Mom is the only one in the family who still uses the nicknames, but neither my brother nor I will ever correct her.

"When does everyone else arrive?" I ask, knowing it most likely won't just be the four of us for this engagement party.

"Juliana's on her way, but everyone else should arrive in about thirty minutes or so. Everything's ready. Appetizers for food, plenty of wine and beer. Nothing fancy. There will only be fifteen of us or so."

I can't help but raise my eyebrows. "That's it?"

Mom laughs. "Who else do I need here?"

"I thought for sure you'd invite the whole city. When you and Hudson first got together, you threw a dinner to celebrate your new-found love that rivaled a lot of weddings."

I'm treated to another of Mom's laughs. "I figured I should save some of the *wow* factor for my own wedding."

*My own wedding.* I have no idea why those words hit me so hard. I haven't exactly dated with marriage in mind. It's pretty much just been a distant possibility. Somehow, though, Marcy is at the forefront of my thoughts as I think about weddings. She could be my gorgeous date. *She could one day be my gorgeous bride.*

That right there? That's the kind of shit I need to shut down. I can't even get her to tell me why she won't date me anymore. How can I possibly still think about the future with her? Our surprise date was supposed to be a sleigh ride through the woods. I planned on packing blankets, and travel heating pads, and coffee, and maybe a warm picnic for afterward. I also wanted to see if she'd be interested in going to the interactive adventure place or one of those escape rooms I've been to with friends but never a date. I had so many date ideas for us, a first for me. I usually just stick with meals, coffee, drinks, maybe a movie or a night at home or a game. Never have I put so much thought and effort into thinking of things we could try together. I bet she might even like that cooking class Henry and Effie do.

Mom and I make our way to the kitchen to join my brother and Hudson.

"What's up, man?" I greet Henry.

He comes at me with this complicated hand-shake-hug-fist-bump combo we came up with years ago and haven't done in ages. I laugh, knowing this means he's in a really good mood. I'm just as happy for Mom and Hudson as my brother is. Mom and our dad divorced about seven years ago, but things were falling apart between them long before then. So much so that she rarely acknowledged Dad as more than the father of her children. She definitely stopped calling him her husband even when he still held that position, though honestly, it was in name only.

I suppose my parents' divorce should have shaken me to my core, despite being an adult at the time. Before I left for college, I knew there was a deadline on their marriage, and it was definitely not until death parted them. And seeing Mom so happy now? That's the very best thing that could have come out of all of it.

Dad's not a bad guy. He just wasn't attentive. Mom's days, her daily life, didn't matter to him. Her opinions, her beliefs, her dreams—all moot points in his eyes. He loved without loving. I know all the way to my very depths that I could do better than my father in this regard. If I found the right woman, I would love her and dote on her and care about every single aspect of her life. *Why won't Marcy see that?*

For crying out loud.

There I go again.

After the guests start arriving, I pull my brother aside and hand him a cold bottle of beer. We toast them with a clink, then take our first swigs at the same time. "What's up, Wick?" he asks after a quick second sip.

Great. Now Henry is using my nickname, too, which means he suspects something's happened to upset me.

"All good," I tell him, giving my best wide grin.

Of course, he doesn't buy it. His face tells me so, as do his next words. "Seriously, Alec. What's going on with you? You've been moody and sullen all night."

I don't bother suppressing a laugh. "I have not. I've smiled as much as the rest of you."

"Okay, sure you have. Which tells me you're good at faking it. But why do you look like you'd love nothing more than to run out of here when you think no one's looking? And before you call me crazy or put up some lame excuse, Effie noticed, too."

At this, I groan.

"It's about a woman, isn't it?"

I nod. "She works at that flower shop Effie sent me to. I have no idea what the hell happened. I was awkward and nervous with her."

"Which never happens anymore," my brother adds with a laugh. "So vintage Alec showed up, huh?"

"Yeah. We hit it off. Had an amazing date. Then last night, in the middle of our second one, she jumps up and splits."

"Jumps up from . . ." Henry asks with a raised eyebrow.

"Not that. We were eating dinner, having a good conversation. At least, I thought so. Then she ran out."

"You want her back?"

I shake my head, then internally shake my head at the first head shake. "Maybe. I don't know." Who am I trying to kid, though? Of course I want her back. I want to never have lost her.

I lower my voice as two of my mom's friends walk by. "I like this woman more than I've liked any other, even with these feelings developing so quickly. We could be really great together. But I don't know. Something spooked her. She won't say what." After a swig of beer, I continue. "Maybe it's for the best if she won't even give me a chance."

"But is she worth it?"

Marcy is much, much more like Lucy, my best friend Pete's girlfriend—well, whatever she is at the moment—or even my coworker Tess than she is the only other main woman in my life, my demanding, manipulative sort-of-friend Drea. It feels beyond gross and wrong to compare any of the first three amazing women to Drea, but it also feels wrong to compare Marcy to Lucy and Tess. Marcy is more than I could ever hope for in a girlfriend. In a partner. In the person I can honestly imagine seeing every day and never tiring of. She encompasses all of what I want.

"I think so. But if she won't give me a chance, what choice do I have but to let her go?"

# Chapter 7

## Marcy

I CANNOT FREAKING BELIEVE this.

As if this day couldn't get any worse. I mean, Alec texted me three times today, twice in a casual, "hey, what's up?" kind of way and once to ask me to please call him or at least give him a reason why I'm ignoring him and why I won't talk to him anymore—all three of which I obviously disregarded.

I have not been thinking of our date we were supposed to have yesterday. I didn't think about it from the time I woke up yesterday morning until my eyes closed and I finally drifted off to sleep at the end of the night, wondering what kind of surprise he had in mind for me. I haven't thought about it today *at all*. Of course I haven't. So what if I like surprises? So what if I like Alec? So what if I really, really wanted those two things together? None of it can mean anything.

Though, I do have to admit it means enough to put me in a super shitty mood.

Plus, Lourdes closed the shop up early because we have a seriously heavy winter storm on the way with potential for blizzard-like conditions, which completely makes sense, but I hate losing hours. I have bills and loans that need paid off, and losing hours doesn't help me.

And now this. My freaking car. Dead battery? No gas? Bad starter? I have no idea. The engine just won't turn over. There's no sign to tell me why. All my coworkers already left because I volunteered to lock up. I was still working on the very last details I needed to add to a social media post that's going out tomorrow when Lourdes decided it was time to go home. I made her leave and not wait for me, which was completely against her nature. She's probably annoyed with me now.

I'm annoyed with me, too.

No, I'm pissed off at myself, that's what I am.

I have plenty of people to call, but it's damn cold out. I don't want to make anyone come here to help. No one is really on the street or the sidewalks, either. Every other business on this street already looks closed.

And who decides to show up?

The one person I would not have called.

"What's going on?" Alec asks as soon as I reluctantly roll my window down for him. He's in his tan wool coat, but no gloves or hat. It's too cold for him to be out here like that.

"What are you doing here?" I ask in reply. Maybe I shouldn't be surprised to see him, but I am. He had to have just come from work, as he's in suit pants and dress shoes. I can't see what's on top of his muscular torso since his coat is buttoned up. I wonder if his tie still hangs around his neck or if he shoved it into a pocket or tossed it onto the passenger seat of his car. I wish he gave me answers like this.

"Car trouble?"

"How did you even manage to show up here at just the right time?" I really want the answer to this one.

"Are you saying you need me?" This is asked with a sly eyebrow raise.

Gah. It's only been a few days since we saw each other in person or connected in any meaningful way—I obviously don't count the texts I pretended I never got—and boy have I missed this man. I can't hold in a laugh. "Are we seriously only going to speak in questions now?"

"How many more will it take before you break?" he asks, lifting an eyebrow again. I've always been fascinated by the way some people can do that. I can barely lift both of my own. They don't seem to like moving much at all.

"Do you want help or not?" His words sound demanding, but his tone is soft, his voice smooth. I hate how much I've missed hearing him speak.

I nod, then open my door to get out. Alec motions for me to stay in. "It's cold out here. Just tell me what happened."

He and I both know if it weren't for my car, he'd be asking me this same question about us right this moment. "It won't start. I don't know why."

"Do you have enough gas?"

I turn the key enough to read the gauges. "It says I do, but it's been acting up lately. I need to take it to get looked at, but I just haven't had the chance to yet."

Alec is quiet, clearly thinking something serious. There is no hint of a smile anywhere on his face. "That's an important part," he finally says. "Your fuel gauge. You can't just hope it's accurate. Please promise me you'll get it looked at soon."

His sweet kindness has my back sweaty and my lonely arms aching. On our first date, he hugged me goodnight like no one ever has. It was the kind of embrace romance authors would describe with words like *swoon-worthy* and *knee-weakening* and *panty-melting*, and yes, having his arms around me abso-freaking-lutely was all those things and more, but Alec . . . Oh, Alec is all those things on his own, with or without touching me.

I don't verbally answer him. My mouth is too dry and my tongue is too thick. I can only nod. Not sure I even remember what I'm agreeing to, but the depth of his concern has me wanting to say yes to any and everything.

Alec nods once, then instructs me to pop the hood on my car so he can take a look.

"I didn't realize you knew anything about cars," I call to him, finally finding my voice again, my body lifted up enough that I can kind of stick my head out the window.

"I have to at least try. Now get back in there and close your window."

He doesn't say why he has to check the engine. It's clearly more than simply because it isn't working.

I do as he says. When he tells me to try the ignition again, I do that, too. Still doesn't work. Then he adjusts the position of his car and tries giving mine a jump, to no avail. After a few more minutes, Alec returns to my driver's side window. I already have it down, having started it when he was closing the hood.

"You'll probably need to call a towing company or a mechanic. It's getting late, and with the snowstorm coming in, I'm guessing most auto parts stores in the area might shut down for the day."

I heave a sigh. It's exactly what I expected but hoped I wouldn't hear. I should thank him for trying his best. Though he might not realize it, I am so appreciative of him taking the time to help me, even though it came to nothing. Now I have to fight back tears. I hate that my car is broken. I hate that I can't let Alec comfort me despite knowing he would, as evidenced by the kind look in his eyes as he watches me. Still, I don't ask for the thing I now need most.

"Want a ride?" Alec offers.

I know he said *a ride* and not *to ride*, but this doesn't stop the tingles from forming all over my body. I'm stuck with only nods for answers again as he also asks if I was on my way home.

After grabbing my bag and hat from my passenger seat, I lock my car and step over to Alec's. This reminds me of the story I read in my new journal of how Wick once helped a stranded family when their car broke down in a thunderstorm and there was a warning for flash flooding. All the stories I've read about Wick have shown him to be kind and caring and intelligent. All the traits Alec shares with him. But when the similarities end with *likes computers* versus *likes sports*, I know that Alec just can't be the one. Even if he is here rescuing me during a major winter storm, despite my avoidance of him these past three days.

I don't open the passenger-side door on his car. Alec got there before me. He stands next to it, one hand on the door and one reaching out to help me into my new seat. I stand on the snowy asphalt, gazing into his eyes, hand in his, unable to pull myself away from his touch, even if it is temporary. Even if I'm the one who put a stop to this before it became anything. Well, anything bigger than I already feel, which is way more than I should.

"It's pretty windy, Marce," Alec says before moving his eyes toward the car.

I hold steady, admiring his face, though the wind whips my hair around. He's gone a bit scruffy, clearly not having shaved in the several days since I last saw him.

"Marce?" He gives my hand a little shake.

The lightly falling snow is no longer light. "Alec." His name is barely more than a whisper on my lips.

His cheeks are already pink from the cold. I can't tell if my sudden inability to hide my true feelings has any effect on him.

But Alec shakes his head and says gruffly, "Get in the car, Marce. We need to get you home." And the moment is over. Only I like this side of him as much as I like his awkwardness. I want every version of Alec.

Too bad the biggest part of him is still the one I can't overlook.

He is probably crazy obsessed with sports, watching games *all the time, I assume,* and I know I'm assuming and have had zero proof to back this up this yet I think it anyway—which means he'll never fully be available to me or for me, I also safely assume.

Well, I think it's a reasonable assumption.

How can it be wrong? It makes sense. I can't do that again. It' s far too painful to play second fiddle to a freaking *game*.

Once Alec pulls up to the main entrance of my apartment building, I've already got my seat belt off, and I'm pulling on the door handle.

"At least let me put the damn car into park," he huffs, putting his foot on the brake.

I'm being reckless, and I don't care. I want to climb over the center console and into Alec's arms, which tells me I have to run up to my apartment and lock the door behind me. This man will only abandon me for a game one day. It will happen. There's no use in explaining it to him. He'll deny it and deny it, until one day it's, *sorry, babe, but these tickets are important to me.* Then what the hell am I? Sorry, *babe*, but I've been there, done that. Never doing it again.

And I know—I *know*—it's Dipshit Dane's voice in my head, not Alec's. I know this. But still, I run.

"Marcy," Alec chides, but it's too late. My purse strap catches on the top corner of the open car door, yanking me back as I run toward the building. Suddenly, I'm on the ground, my legs and feet crumpled beneath me.

"Marcy," Alec says again, only this time it's in distress of a different kind. With the car fully stopped, he jumps out and runs over to me. Well, I assume it's his firm hands on my arms gently guiding me to sit upright. My bare hands are ice cold and have bits of broken pavement stuck on the palms from where the lot got plowed. With the snow already here and more on its way, this pavement will only be visible for another few minutes tops.

"You're only here because my car wouldn't start," I say before he has a chance to speak.

"I didn't know that when I left Syracuse to come to the Falls," he retorts, but he uses such a kind tone that hot tears prick my eyes. Why does he have to be so perfect in every other way? Why can't he be this amazing *indoors* kind of guy?

The snow has picked up even just in the few minutes we've been sitting in the parking lot. Literally. I planted my ass on the pavement in an effort to give my knees a break, but neither position is very comfortable. I refuse Alec's offered hand to help me to my feet. Honestly, I'm a little afraid my left ankle might be twisted. If I say this, or anything else at all, I know for sure the tears will fall. I can't let them.

Alec stands. I think he's on his way to his car, but I don't look to make sure. I don't like the feeling the idea of his departure gives me. It's far too akin to heartbreak, like the way I've felt since I forced myself to leave his apartment three days ago. Then suddenly, hands are under my armpits and I'm on my unsteady feet.

"Stop being so stubborn." Alec's voice barely registers above a whisper.

"If I tell you I'm fine, would you believe me?"

"Just the fact that you're asking tells me you're not."

I wish I had an argument all ready to go against this reply, but I don't.

"Let's get you upstairs," he says.

If it weren't for the circumstances, I'd be putty in his hands right now. One arm is wrapped around my back, his hand on my waist. The other has hold of my arm, which he's draped across his muscled shoulders. Even through the bulk of his coat and his suit jacket, I can feel the physical strength of him. I don't care that I've known him for all of five days. Alec is absolutely the kind of man who could hold me properly and never worry that I'd want him to let me go, because I wouldn't. Ever.

This is the absolute worst.

## Chapter 8

*Alec*

MARCY AND I HOBBLE our way into her apartment building and down the short hall. The hall might not be long, but it's a slow walk. I'm holding as much of her weight as I can to help lessen the pain on her hurt ankle. I start us for the stairs, but then Marcy pulls away. She nearly knocks me off-balance as I adjust my stance to keep us both upright.

"Where are you going?" I demand.

She doesn't answer. She only points to the window that faces opposite her. It's nothing but white.

The snow. Snow squall, in fact. I knew this was a possibility. Everyone around here did. The snow rate increased as Marcy sat on her cute bottom outside in the frozen parking lot and fought back the tears she so clearly needs—or at least needed—to let go of.

"Let's get upstairs," I say, unable to comment on what's brewing outside. I don't know how this is going to go. I'll have to fight my way out of here on the roads. If Marcy's car hadn't broken down, or if I'd been able to start the "can we give this thing between us another chance" conversation sooner, I don't think I'd be in this mess. I would have either been almost home already, or Marcy would be willing to let me stay. As it is, I'm screwed.

I brace her body with my hands and guide her up the staircase, closer and closer to her third-floor apartment. At her door, Marcy digs her keys out of her bag—leaning against me for balance—then unlocks the door and opens it for both of us. I help her hobble over to sit on her sofa. Once she's comfortably down, I step back. Her eyes are trained on her windows, uncovered by the yellow-green curtains hanging off to the sides.

"It's happening too fast. There's going to be too much dumped at once."

"It isn't a surprise," I say. I meant for my voice to be softer than it comes out. "The only thing I'm surprised about right now is you."

Now her eyes flick to gaze at my face, but then she looks away again. "I don't know what you mean."

"Sure, Marce." I know she hears the biting sarcasm in my tone because she flinches. I didn't mean to hurt her with my words. I just want the truth from her, and she's unwilling to give me that.

I step back a little more and make my way to the attached kitchen. After grabbing a bag of frozen peas—the closest thing she has to ice or an ice pack—and the kitchen towel lying on the counter, I return to Marcy. I see she still hasn't elevated her ankle. I kneel down in front of her and lift her foot. There's enough space between her and one of the small pillows that I assume she won't be using it, so I place that under her ankle before setting her foot on the coffee table. Then I pick up the peas and towel from where I left them on the table, wrap the peas up, and place the whole thing on her ankle. "Leave that on for a while."

She doesn't say anything to me.

It's been a couple minutes since I checked the weather. I walk over to one of the windows to watch the heavy falling snow. There's little more to see than a sheet of solid white. "If I knew anyone who lived in this complex, I'd ask to stay with them. I'm sorry I can't change this."

Marcy doesn't reply.

I pull out my phone. Lucy—Pete's girl—lives here in town, but it would be beyond awkward to ask her at the moment. If I remember correctly, the sister of one of my friend's lives around here. I've never visited—haven't actually seen her for years—but if it will put Marcy at ease, I'm willing to ask for help from them. I send off a text, knowing at some point, I have to face Marcy again.

A reply text comes almost immediately.

Barker: Brynley said you can definitely stay with her and her husband if you need to, for as long as you need to. Just give her a call when you're on your way over. But it's a mess out there, man. Stay put if you can.

Stay put?

Not my decision to make.

Then Barker sends another text with the address. Brynley's house is only a few blocks away. I could walk that. Might be safer, or at least easier, than trying to drive over.

I want to walk back to Marcy. Be close enough to gauge the expression on her face as I tell her the news—not that this apartment is large. It's difficult to see her when I'm faced away from her, but my body won't turn and my feet won't move. "A friend of mine has a sister who lives nearby. Really close. I'm going to go stay with them tonight. At least until the worst of this passes."

Marcy doesn't answer. I have to turn to face her to make sure she heard me. Her eyes are wide, and her cheeks are pink. Then her phone beeps. She looks down at it, then back to me.

"I've been getting these alerts all day. Winter storm warning. Blizzard warning. Snow squall. Now the roads are officially closed. You're not going anywhere."

I can't tell if she means she doesn't want me to or if she just means I physically can't because of the weather. "Closed roads don't matter. I can walk."

I watch Marcy's jaw literally falls open. Then she blinks really fast quite a few times. "Alec, it's dangerous out there. You're not leaving."

I'm half elation, half frustration right now. Does she have any idea what she's doing to me? "I can't be here if you don't want me here. I'll only stay if you ask me to."

Marcy leans forward, pulls off the makeshift ice pack, and stands.

Now my feet are in motion. I immediately step over to her. "Hey, put that back on. You need to make sure the swelling doesn't get too bad."

Marcy waves this thought away. "I'm fine. My ankle doesn't hurt that much anymore. Just a slight twist."

I put my hands on my hips, hoping she isn't lying to me.

"Look." She points at the window. "It's a snow squall. It developed rapidly, and with the wind, it's basically a blizzard out there, too."

"I know. I knew it was coming. I've been watching it. It's all the news channels could talk about. All the news headlines said there would be a snowstorm today. That's why I came out to see you. I wanted to make sure you'd be okay in this mess."

Huh. Never thought I'd see a blush on confident Marcy's cheeks. It's pretty. Then she shakes her head, almost like she's trying to shake her complexion back to normal. "I assumed you only wanted to talk about our relationship again. I already gave you my answer to that."

Hearing her call what we had or have a relationship speeds up my heart, despite the words that came after. Maybe I do mean more to her than she's letting on. Or maybe she sees every date as a mini-relationship and I'm nothing special to her.

"What do you say, Marce?" I don't move, my eyes on her, waiting for her reply.

After a few false alarms, she finally speaks. "Please stay."

I give her a quick nod. It's not even close to the bare minimum of what I'd like to do. I want to scoop her into my arms and give her a kiss. I want to hold her and promise to keep her warm through all this. I want to carry her back to the sofa and set her down, replacing the ice on her ankle just in case before curling into her and holding her hand while we watch the snow.

After sending a short "I'm sorry but thanks anyway" text to my friend's sister, and a slightly longer one letting him know I'll explain in more detail later—adding that I'll let them both know if the situation changes again—I remove my coat, tossing it onto her coffee table, then put my phone in my suit pocket before refocusing on Marcy.

"How long have we been here?" she asks.

I check my phone. "Upstairs? About half an hour."

"Not long," she replies.

Something in me says to watch her eyes and face. "Is it too long for you?"

She rolls her eyes slightly. "Alec—"

"Seriously," I interrupt, hoping she'll forgive that. "We didn't even make it through dinner before you took off the other night. I need to know how much you don't want me here right now."

"I told you that you can stay."

I shake my head. "Not the same thing."

Somehow, Marcy and I have made our way closer to each other. Only a few inches separate us. "I want you here." Her voice is barely above a whisper. "I want you, Alec." She gently emphasizes every word.

This puts me into action. My hands are around her, splayed across her back. I lean forward and softly plant a kiss on the spot just above her collarbone. Then I plant another kiss just above that. Marcy gives a hushed moan, her fingers gripping on to my biceps. She pulls me a bit closer. And my phone goes off, the sound of a text from my brother. It's the "Charge" tune often played at games. It's also perfect for Henry since we almost never attend or watch games without one another.

Marcy's fingers tighten more, but it's a lot less pleasant this time. She's almost hurting me. "You need to get that."

"Just my brother," I whisper from her neck, giving her a few short kisses, on my way up to her jaw. "He can wait."

"Check it," she says again, but her voice almost sounds like she's being strangled.

I pull back. "Why? What's wrong? What's happening?" I try to catch her gaze, but she won't look me in the eye. "Marce?"

The lights go out. It's suddenly very quiet, telling me the refrigerator is no longer running its cycle, either. I don't have to wonder. The electricity is out. Possibly a wide blackout, based on the weather.

I can tell Marcy realizes this, too.

"You have to go," she says, her eyes wild, her skin pale.

"What do you mean?" I feel my brows shift together. "Is everything okay? Does your ankle hurt again?" I know I'm grasping at straws. I know it. But something changed in less than a minute, and I can't for the life of me figure out what it is and how to fix it.

"You have to go." Marcy keeps repeating this.

She slips out of my grasp and is . . . out the damn door again.

Damn it.

I run after her, grabbing her keys before closing her door, just so she doesn't end up locked out. She's fast, though, even with a twisted ankle. It has to be better, because I can't imagine her being able to sprint like that otherwise. Finally, I find her in the shroud of snow, digging out my already buried car with her bare hands. I wrench her up and take her hands in mine. "What the hell are you doing? Do you want to get frostbite?" She doesn't even have her coat. While I'm no longer wearing mine, I do have my suit jacket on. However, I'm afraid if I let her go to take it off for her, she'll break away from me and return to her digging.

"You have to go," she tells me yet again.

"Why?" I snap, but not out of anger. I'm just confused. "Marce, talk to me. Why do I have to leave? What changed?"

Her eyes are teary. Not a good thing out here in these conditions.

I take a risk and pull her into me, wrapping my open coat around her as much as possible, sharing my body heat.

"You're only going to hurt me," she adds in a small voice.

I . . . I don't have an immediate answer to this. *What?* She thinks . . . she thinks I'll *hurt* her?

Marcy is completely safe with me. How does she not know that? I would never, *ever* hurt her or anyone. I try to hold her and warm her up with my body heat while finding words that won't come out sounding like a wounded animal, even though that's how I feel. She has wounded me to my core. The fact that she thinks I'll hurt her? It doesn't sit right with me at all.

But Marcy slips away again. She's too damn wiggly to hold on to. She takes off around my car. I stumble after her in these damn dress shoes, hoping I can keep her from falling, but she's out of reach. I slip in the snow and grab on to my car for balance. Then Marcy shrieks again. It sounds exactly the same as it did when her purse strap caught on my car door and she fell earlier. I say so many curse words in my head and out loud as I make my way to her as fast as I can. "Marcy!"

I find her lying in the snow on the opposite side of me, on her hip this time. "Will you please stop running from me? I promise I will never hurt you. Let me help you."

She reaches her hands up to me. I bend toward her and lift, but stop when she cries out. I'm immediately down on my knees, wrapping her up in me again. "What's injured?"

"My hip." She shifts her body and cries out once more.

Shit. "How bad is it? Do you need an ambulance?" Syracuse Falls is tiny, but in this weather, it might take them a while to get here.

"I don't think so. It's going to be a hell of a bruise, though."

I hate hearing the pain in her voice. She clutches me closer, her teary eyes devolving into full-blown sobs. Slowly, I stroke a hand up and down her back, keeping the other one completely wrapped around her. "It's okay. I've got you. This will probably make it difficult to walk, but we'll go up like we did before, okay?"

I feel her nod.

"If at any point it hurts too much, just let me know and we'll take a few seconds, or even minutes, if you need to pause before going again."

"All right."

I lean close to her ear. "I promise I'm going to take care of you."

She nods again then we tighten our grip on each other and rise to our feet.

# Chapter 9

## Alec

MARCY DOESN'T TENSE IN my arms. That's the first thing I notice as we stand in her apartment again, warming up together. She doesn't flinch at my touch. If she's afraid of me, it isn't physically. She isn't worried about violence, but the fact that I have to stand here and actually ascertain this breaks my heart a little.

"I will never hurt you," I tell her again, the flashlight on my phone enveloping us in bright light.

She only shakes her head, tears still spilling out of her eyes.

"Marce, talk to me please. Just tell me what the hell is going on in that beautiful mind of yours. Tell me what you're afraid of."

"We have to get out of our wet clothes," she says instead, and damn it, I hate how right she is. Even if she is cleverly using it as an opportunity to change the subject.

"Okay. Let's get you to your room."

I don't have anything to change into, but maybe I'll air-dry, I think. Suit pants can't stay wet forever, right? Without electricity, and clearly no backup generators since nothing is working, no heat will kick on. But it'll be fine. No sense in distressing Marcy with thoughts of me walking around here in my boxer briefs. The suit stays on.

After grabbing my phone to help us see, I guide Marcy to her open bedroom doorway, then over to her dresser. She leans on me for support as she digs out leggings and a stretchy tank top. No bra or underwear. I have to cough just to make myself breathe again. As it is, I'm not sure I'm swallowing. All I'm doing is drowning in happy, lustful thoughts of Marcy leaning her body against me with only one thin layer between me and all the rest of her.

I clear my throat, determined to fight those mental pictures. It isn't right to do that while holding her. She's let me know in many ways that she isn't interested in me, or at the very least, that she doesn't trust me. Trust is a huge deal for Marcy, and without hers, we will never get to that point.

She digs in another drawer, one down toward the floor. I have to help her bend down there and stand back up. Marcy comes back with another handful of clothes and pushes them toward me. I look down at the items she holds. Looks like a T-shirt and a faded pair of sweatpants, presumably my size. She wouldn't give me something that belonged to *him*, would she? What would it mean if she did? That she's still hung up on him? That she couldn't bear to let go of his things? That she forgot about them until now and it's all she has that'll fit me? No way in hell will I ever wear a freaking thing that was once her jackass ex-boyfriend's.

I haven't touched the proffered clothes yet. "If those are Dipshit Dane's, I'm walking out of here right now."

Marcy casually shakes her head. "It's my brother's stuff. I borrowed them the last time I crashed at his house, around Thanksgiving. I haven't seen him for a while because we're both busy with our jobs. He was also sick during Christmas. It's okay for you to wear them."

For a moment, I stare back down at the shirt and sweats, then back up at her beautiful face.

"I promise I would never offer you anything that was Dipshit Dane's. That's just cruel and not fair to you."

And I believe her. I keep one hand on her side, holding her steady, and use the other to gently take the clothes from her hand. "Will you need help changing out of your wet things?" I'm shocked this didn't come out in a babbling mess. The idea of helping Marcy strip down to nothing and cover back up in not a whole lot, to be honest, has my forehead sweaty. We are adults. I should be able to handle this just fine. But all I can think of is how nice it will feel to have her bare skin on mine, as transient as the moment will be.

Marcy slowly spins around to face me, her clothes in the crook of one elbow. "Alec, I—" She stops herself short and scrubs a hand over her face.

"It's okay. Whatever it is, I'll do my best to make it better for you."

She blinks several times then locks her gaze on my eyes. "Apart from physically needing you here—because damn it, I need you to take care of me even though part of me still wants to insist I'm fine—I genuinely *want* you here." She almost shudders as she speaks, but the soft groan that comes with it tells me that the shudder isn't from horror or disgust. Marcy's thinking *things*.

I catch a glimpse of the pink now spreading on her cheeks. Marcy gently pushes me back a little, I'm guessing to move us away from the dresser. But I stumble back, she trips, and her empty hand grabs the first thing within reach. There's an odd, muted sort of noise, then the unmistakable sound of one of my shirt's buttons clattering on the floor. I hold us both up on our feet. No more falling allowed—only every move of this woman has me falling harder for her.

One look at Marcy's wide, guilty eyes, and I'm chuckling. "Don't worry about it. My dry cleaner will fix it."

We glance around for a few seconds, realizing we don't know where the button even went. Marcy's face has fallen into a frown as she looks at me again. "Hey, it's okay." I toss both stacks of dry clothes over onto her bed, which is closer than I initially thought. Then I wrap my arms around her in a tight hug.

Once again, Marcy does not tense up in my embrace. In fact, she's relaxed into me so much that I wonder if maybe she's getting tired. I have no idea how early she woke up this morning or how much she slept last night.

When we finally pull away from each other, Marcy starts shivering. Right. Wet clothes. No working furnace.

"Ready?" I ask, my eyebrows raised, hoping she'll get what I mean without additional words.

She does. "Yeah."

This one word is just raspy and seductive enough to send a shiver through my body. I'm about to see Marcy Haskens naked. Marcy guides me over to the bed, though I'm still supporting her. She leans one hip against the side of the mattress and gently tugs my right hand to hold on to her other hip. Within seconds, Marcy's top half is covered only by a dark blue bra. I glance down at her pants.

"How do you want to do this?" I ask, trying to keep as much headiness out of my voice as possible. She doesn't need to know how turned on I am. That wouldn't be fair to her.

Then her eyes go dark, her pupils dilated. "Lay me on the bed. On my back. That should be easiest."

Right. Sure. Easiest thing in the world. Lay this incredible woman on her bed and remove her pants like it means nothing to me and to her, because I'm still not sure how she feels about me and all this. Turned on is one thing. Falling as hard and fast as I am is another. I can only hope she's with me on this.

But now's not the time.

Slowly, carefully, I lean Marcy's body back with my arms and hands, mindful of her injured hip, eventually landing her on top of her messy bed. After a quick adjustment, Marcy looks up at me expectantly. She can't bend to remove her own pants, as that would put too much pressure on her hip. I take a deep breath and let it out as quietly as I can before peeling her damp leggings down her hips and off her legs, Marcy moving her body as needed to give me better access. Suddenly, she's only in her bra and a dark blue lace thong.

Then she tugs at one side of the thong. "This should go, too. It's still wet from the first time I was on my bottom in the parking lot."

I force myself to stay in total control of my actions and reactions. No surprises allowed. I carefully slip it off of her, averting my gaze from what I know she doesn't want me to see. Turning for a moment, I grab her clean maroon leggings off the folded-over sheet and ready them for a ride up her glorious legs. Between the two of us, the leggings make it to her knees. Then Marcy uses me to pull herself up to those knees and finishes pulling the bottoms all the way over her ass to the lower edge of her waist.

Since she's situated enough to be able to put her tank top on herself, I turn and undo the remaining buttons on my dress shirt. Off goes my suit jacket, then my shirt. I think I hear Marcy gasp, but when I spin and face her, she's looking away from me. "Everything okay?" I ask.

"Fine." Except her voice is extra breathy. And her top still isn't on.

I shift away again and slip my dress pants off. My socks didn't get wet, but I'd rather remove them anyway. After I pull the sweatpants up enough to cover my underwear, I turn again to catch Marcy watching me. She still isn't wearing her tank top, just her bra and leggings. Her cheeks are so pink now, I think maybe I don't need those flowers of the same color every day. I just need this. I need her.

I move to grab the T-shirt she's lending me, but then she bends and pulls it out of my reach.

"What's going on, Marce?" My voice is as breathy as hers.

"I was thinking."

"Good or bad?"

She smiles at my flirty tone. "Body heat. People say to use skin-on-skin for the most body heat to stay warm and not freeze to death. We have no idea how long the power outage will last. I also don't have that many blankets here. So I'm thinking we just leave our shirts off." She pauses. "You tell me if that's good or bad."

Hearing her use that same flirty tone I used has me biting back against a moan desperate to escape. I open my mouth to speak, but then she says, "And if it's skin-on-skin we need, this"—she tugs at her bra strap—"will only get in the way."

If the sight of Marcy in only a bra wasn't enough of a temptation, she's now completely topless in front of me. I dutifully keep my gaze on her eyes, but her gaze wanders down my body and back up. She beckons me to join her on the bed, and I desperately miss my long wool coat right now. Well, I miss what that coat could hide on me. But then we are snuggled together under her blankets and sheets, arms wrapped around each other, legs intertwined, and I can't even remember what that stupid coat looks like.

# Chapter 10

## Marcy

WICK MADE THE DEAN'S list, and he volunteered with charities. Wick traveled the world, or at least to parts of it, and most of the US. What do I know about Alec? He works with mortgages and likes sports. That's all there is to him, as far as I can tell. If there's more, wouldn't he be willing to tell me? Wouldn't he be eager to share more of that with me?

And yes, I know he's kind, and helpful. And so damn caring. He followed me out into the snow twice just to make sure I was okay.

I tried not to let that get to me. Tried to think maybe that didn't matter. Maybe he did what any other human would have done.

Then he looks at me. It's more than his handsome face or his brilliant smile. More than the glow in his cheeks or the spark in his eyes. He wants me in every way. This isn't just a fling to him, or it wouldn't be if I'd just let him in. We are naked from the waist up. My idea, yes. My own personal torment. Get his skin on me and pretend it means nothing close to what it really does, all the while acting like I couldn't care less. Stupid, stupid woman. That's me.

We should be back to back, or at least back to chest. His chest, not mine. There is no reason that Alec and I are face to face—meaning chest to chest—right now. Well, no reason involving the excuse

I used to get him shirtless in my bed, even if it included me being shirtless, too.

Lourdes's best friend fell in love with her now-husband like this. Well, I can't say for sure that they were naked in any way. Not my business. But they were stranded in a blizzard and got to know each other well enough to know they never wanted to be apart. That can't possibly happen for me, though.

"I am *not* Gwenn."

"I know that," Alec says slowly. "You're Marcy. Did you think I forgot your name?" His face is scrunched.

"No, I know. I didn't mean to say that out loud."

"What do you mean?"

*This is all too perfect.* That's what I mean. *You're too charming and too alluring and too kind and far too endearing. I cannot fall for another die-hard sports fanatic.* But I don't say this. I won't. Because, honestly, I'm not sure I mean it. I *am* falling hard for him. I've fallen so damn far now that I can't even remember where I started. Alec isn't too much of anything. He's just the right amount of everything.

"I can't fall in love with you just because we are stranded together by a snowstorm and you're taking care of me." I doubt he has any idea what I'm talking about. He's probably never even met Gwenn.

"Fair enough. What would need to happen in order for you to fall in love with me?"

Oh no. I'm not telling him that. There's only one requirement: hate sports. That's not going to happen. The best I can do is get a little closer to this answer than my instincts are telling me to. "Dipshit Dane ruined me."

Alec cocks his head. His hand on my bare waist burns my skin in the most pleasurable way. "You aren't an eighteenth-century spinster. No one can *ruin* you."

"You'd be surprised." I give a sardonic laugh. "He's the only man who ever convinced me to kiss on the first date."

Alec shifts his body at this, his face telling me he'd rather have his nails chewed off by a shark one by one than hear about me kissing another man.

"Got me into bed on the first date, too. I had never, *ever* moved that fast before, and I haven't since. Well, until now. Until you." I pause. "Dane told me he loved me on our second date, and I believed him. But he was all wrong for me. I didn't know how wrong until it was well beyond fixing or getting out unscathed."

At this, Alec nods, acknowledging how important this moment is. Then he says slowly, "I'm not Dipshit Dane. I don't know what he did to you . . ."

And yes, I am absolutely regretting my decision to not tell him about the worst breakup in history, but it's still too mortifying to relive to the most amazing man I've ever met.

". . . but I swear I'm not going anywhere unless you want me to. Even then, I might be tempted to make it hard for you to shake me." He gives me a sly grin. "Though you're more than welcome to shake me in other ways." Then he freaking winks. I can't remember the last time a man winked at me. It's just as heart-melting as I'd expect it to be. Add in the fact that we're currently half-nude and also that he can feel my breasts on him, and I'm a complete mess.

Neither of us are breathing normally. Neither of us have steady heartbeats.

The temptation is too great. But is it really a temptation if two people both want it desperately and there is no logical reason why they can't have it? There is nothing stopping us from taking each other in every way that we want, apart from my stupidly terrified mind. But with every passing moment, I see more and more how Alec could be the one I want, perhaps forever.

"What was the surprise you had in mind for us? For yesterday's date, I mean."

That same half-smile pulls at his lips like Thursday night when he first asked me about it. "If things go well, don't you still want to be surprised by it?"

I do. I really do. But something in me is desperate to know what he thinks might be an ideal date with me. "Please tell me."

Alec kisses my temple, then slowly, softly strokes his thumb on my arm. Our cocoon under the blankets has us toasty warm. "I planned to take you on a sleigh ride in the woods."

"Oh." Not my idea of a great time, honestly, being out in nature. I'm not sure if my face is expressing the not-quite-happy surprise I feel.

Then Alec continues. "I was going to pack several blankets, one of those cordless, cloth heating mats so our asses don't get too cold, and hot cinnamon coffee, the way you ordered it the other night. Then I thought we could have a picnic afterward. We'd still have the warm blankets and mat, and we could pack hot foods."

"Oh." This time this word is much softer, much more understanding. The date would have been so much more than just being outside. He put a lot of thought into that date. Now more than ever, I regret that it didn't happen.

I pull his arms tighter around me, then lean in and gently graze my lips across the side of his jaw.

"Are you sure you want this, Marce?"

He doesn't even need me to explain it to him. Alec knows exactly what I'm doing. I hope I can find the right words to tell him why. "I haven't slept with anyone in about two years. It's a choice I don't make often."

With a shake of his head, Alec says, "Me either. It's been almost a year."

"I want you, Alec. All of you. Please."

At that last word, he shifts our bodies, sliding his hands down from my back to press my pelvis into his. I can now feel his excitement as well as my own. He pauses a moment, moving away just enough so we can make eye contact.

"How do your gorgeous hips feel?"

"Like there's not a thing wrong with them," I whisper, dipping my head to plant a quick kiss on his chin.

Alec moves his head so my lips miss his chin and land on his mouth. We start off softly, as I hadn't expected this kiss so soon. Then I grip his back, pressing my fingers into his skin, and our kiss deepens to an intensity I've never had with any man before, not even Dane. I don't notice if Alec tastes like mint or fruit or soda or even his lunch from earlier today. What I really notice is that his kiss tastes like the kind of kiss I want every morning when I wake up and every night before I go to sleep. He tastes like feelings I was determined to squash for all of eternity for no damn good reason.

I take my time sliding a hand down his smooth, muscular back until I reach the waistband of his sweatpants. When I give it a tug, Alec pulls back again to look at me, practically panting.

"I don't feel any pain," I tell him, taking hold of his top arm, removing it from my back. In one long, deliberate motion, I glide his fingertips across my skin from my waist, around and up to my ribs, then up farther still, to one of the softest, silkiest parts of me.

Alec's eyes take in where I've placed his hand. He leans to kiss me there, then returns to my mouth, his breath warm on me. "How would you like to test those hips with me to be sure?"

And once again, the most perfect man has asked the most perfect question.

# Chapter 11

## Marcy

THERE IS A NAKED man in my bed.

That's the first thing that comes to mind as I lie here Wednesday morning.

The electricity is still out. The heat can't kick on without power. I have water, but it's far too cold to shower with. And I've had a naked man in my bed for almost fourteen hours now.

Alec shifts his body, adjusting the arm he has draped around me so he can pull me a little closer to him. I wouldn't dare resist. It's far too wonderful being here like this with him. Even when the dipshit actually pretended to love me, we never cuddled like this. He liked going home after, or sending me on my way. Claimed he snored too loud and was "afraid" I'd break up with him over it. Didn't matter that it wasn't always the right time of day for sleeping. Alec, though, he is all about the snuggles.

My back is to him, but after the light kiss he drops on my shoulder, I roll to face him. He keeps his left arm on me the whole time, never losing that sizzling contact. "Hey," I say, relaxing my head down on his right bicep. It's seriously the perfect pillow. This is the third time I've done so since last night, and Alec has smiled wide every time.

He's already grinning as he moves toward me for a kiss. It's soft and quick, but still full of the heady passion we spent at least half the night expressing.

"Good morning," he whispers. "Or is it afternoon?"

I laugh. "Still morning. Right around ten." Then I kiss him again, just a whisper of one on his lips. I never thought I'd reach a point when I desperately want my lips on a man *all the time*, yet here I am.

Alec didn't have to come out to the Falls with a snowstorm looming. Even after showing up, he could have just dropped me off at home then left. He could have went to his friend's house. He could have slept on the sofa instead of in here with me. Everything he's done for me these past twenty-four hours, when looked at separately, are kind enough. Put all of them together? It makes him the best man I've ever known or could hope to know. Right now, I choose to ignore the one and only thing I don't like about him. It has no place in this moment.

"How cold do you think it'll get?" I'm not sure if he's wondered this yet, but it's something I can't stop thinking about. Late last night, I received a text sent to all the tenants of Apple Lane Apartments that the management was struggling to get the generators operational. As far as I can tell, they still aren't working.

"Not sure," he says. "Hopefully not too bad. I guess it depends on how long the blackout lasts, how well insulated this building is, the temperature of the room before the electricity cut off and how much heat it's held on to, and if they are able to get the generators started. I don't think we're anywhere near seeing our breath."

There's a lot of science and math involved in that answer, which I simultaneously adore and am surprised at. However, I'd much rather focus on the kisses Alec is pressing along my exposed shoulder. Then he pulls the blanket up and back over me, leaving only my head visible.

"I've never been snowed in like this before," he tells me.

"I have, but never here. The last time this happened to me, I still lived with my parents." After yawning, I realize we'll have to find things to keep us occupied. Otherwise, we might be tempted to sleep a lot, which probably wouldn't be good for our circadian rhythms. "What would you like to do today?" I ask after he plants a kiss above my right eyebrow.

He dramatically wiggles his own eyebrows at me with a huge grin.

I can't help but laugh. "Other than that."

"What do you have here?" he asks, a little more serious.

Most of what I like to do is on the computer. My desktop has a whole bunch of games downloaded onto it, but that's no use now. My laptop has plenty of battery life left, but there's no internet or Wi-Fi thanks to the power outage. I have a few crossword puzzle and other word game books. I also have lots of board games and plenty of shelves full of books. But I'm apprehensive about discussing this. Alec is all about sports. He's never mentioned just hanging out at home doing anything other than watching a game or match on TV. What if he laughs at me when I tell him what the options are?

"What would you do if you were at home?"

Alec lifts his left hand and brushes the many stray hairs out of my face. "Maybe play with Crunch. Text my friends or my brother. Go out for a walk if it wasn't too bad or over to my neighbor's place. He has a foosball table and a pool table."

Of course. Why am I not surprised his answer includes the very thing I'm trying not to think about?

"Right. Sadly, all I can offer you are novels, puzzle books, and board games."

"And you."

He kisses my forehead at my confused expression. "I very much like talking with you," he adds. "If you put your clothes back on and decide we're no longer doing what we've been doing, I'll still be happy to be here talking with you. Just so long as you don't shut me out."

I bite my bottom lip, trying to get a read on him. "You'd be okay with zero sex from here on out?"

"I'd be sad, yes. I'd wonder if there was a good reason or if I did something wrong. But again, so long as you don't shut me out and push me away, I'd be thrilled to still be here with you conversing with you, watching you, being near you. I like you, Marce."

"I like you, too," I whisper back. I can't seem to say more. No man has ever given me such a sweet, honest speech before. My heart is tempted to add more. *I'll fall in love with you if I let myself.* I tell it to shut up right now. It's *way* too soon for that.

Only a few more seconds pass before I make up my mind and scoot closer to him. I angle my body so I can kiss Alec's chest and neck, something I discovered last night he likes more than almost anything. Then my stomach grumbles. Alec chuckles, then looks down my body before making eye contact again. "I think we need to raid the pantry first."

Though I don't pull away, I do admit he's probably right. Then I add, "I can't make any promises that there's anything more than strawberry toaster pastries, cheese crackers, jarred salmon, and peanut butter in my cabinets."

Alec tilts my chin up so I catch his gaze. "Sounds like a perfect meal."

As long as I'm with him, it always will be.

# Chapter 12

## Alec

THE GORGEOUS WOMAN IN bed with me shifts her body, but I know she's not trying to scoot away from me. We haven't extracted ourselves from each other for the last three hours at least. I assume it's still Thursday, but I'm not entirely sure. It might be Friday already. Hell, it could be next Tuesday, and I would neither know nor care.

Marcy's bare back is up against my chest. My left arm is around her waist, with my hand splayed on her stomach. My other arm is her pillow. The clothes she pulled out of the dresser on Tuesday lie discarded somewhere on the floor, as do the clothes we'd been wearing before all that. Whenever we've had to leave this bed—mostly for food, water, and bathroom breaks—we've done so naked or wrapped in one of the fluffy, Marcy-sized novelty blankets she found folded in a messy stack in her closet.

The electricity has been back on for most of the day now, and we've finally been able to shower again—the water, though still usable, was far too cold—and crank the thermostat to scorching. Here, under the covers, it's much, much hotter.

Now that I've seen all of Marcy, I can't go back to my life the way it was before she came along. I don't want to. The Alec I was didn't have the privilege of knowing of the beauty, magnificence, and strength of Marcy Haskens. I don't want to be anywhere else. I'm definitely not ready to leave. Not sure I ever will be. I don't think Marcy wants me to go, either. Every time I move the slightest bit, even if I have to shift away for a moment to get more comfortable, she pulls me back to her, grumbling in that sexy way she has about not letting me go.

Only two days ago, neither of us was sure she even wanted me here. I didn't know if she still had feelings for me. I hoped, but hope can only do so much.

I don't need to worry now. She isn't running away anymore. She isn't hiding herself behind her fears. For the moment, I'm choosing to embrace the warm, cuddly side of her and ignore the fact that she still won't tell me what exactly those fears are.

My phone beeps, but I don't want to look at it. Instead, I lean forward and breathe a soft exhale near Marcy's ear. She tightens the hand that holds my forearm, sending that shock through me that I've come to adore almost as much as I adore her. Then comes that pleased sigh I'm already familiar with. And the moan. It's there right at the end. Not nearly as intense as other certain moments, but still something that kicks my heart into overdrive.

"Is it morning?" she asks, her voice raspy. Well, I did have her screaming out and begging for more not so long ago, so it's no surprise. It didn't seem to matter how much she tried to muffle herself with her pillow. I just hope she wasn't loud enough for any neighbors to hear. I'd hate for her to live with that kind of embarrassment.

"Not sure," I say, now at her neck. I nibble the skin just under my mouth, then move slightly and nibble there, too. Nothing separates her body from mine. I know on her stomach, she can feel how much I'm enjoying this.

"Should we check the time?"

Marcy and I had a whole discussion earlier, starting from when the power came back on. We figured it was time to get back to normal life. According to the alerts on our phones, the roads reopened this morning. Only neither of us wanted to leave her comfortable bed. Neither of us wanted to put clothes back on, either. We'd already talked about the fact that she didn't lose much food to spoilage because of the blackout, mostly because she didn't have a lot in her fridge and freezer to begin with. Her pantry foods sustained us enough, though with all the physical *exercise* she and I did yesterday and today, I'm surprised we aren't starving right now.

We are, however, out of something very important. I should get dressed for that. Well, *those*. I know for a fact Marcy would not only understand, but encourage it. She could stay here cocooned in her blankets, warm and waiting for me . . .

I groan, aching to give us both the thing we want most without having to part from her, not even an inch. And the way Marcy's wiggling, I'm not sure I'll make it out of here with a normal breath, a normal heart rate, and no visible signs of why.

My phone beeps again, and then again.

Now I groan for a new reason. I had to call off work due to the winter storm. It's possible that it's Pete or our friend and co-worker Tess trying to catch me up on all I've missed. Neither of them consider hours of the day when texting. Whoever is texting also isn't considering the possibility that I'm nestled in a naked cocoon with Marcy right now.

She turns and kisses me the way she did last night, right before I almost confessed that I think I'm falling in love with her and that I don't care that it's the craziest thing I've ever done. I roll our bodies, cover her torso with mine, and tell her everything I feel without saying a word, our lips never parting. Eventually, she places a hand on my chin, the sign for me to stop. I pull back and gaze as this gorgeous woman I have the honor of holding in my arms.

We share one last quick kiss, no more than a sweet peck, before rolling out of bed and forcing our bodies into the clothes we haven't really worn in two days. It's been a lot of naked time, both for heat and for other things. This shirt and these pants feel unnatural now. I hate this suit. My favorite suit. Nothing is as comfortable—nothing could ever be as perfect—as Marcy and her blankets on my skin.

Once we are dressed and I've made sure there are no emergent messages on my phone, I pull Marcy to me for a few soft kisses, from her cheek to her forehead to her lips, where I linger before planting several on her neck. "I love that we're back in this again, Marce. Let's make a date. What about the sleigh ride? There'll be more than enough snow for it now."

The laugh she lets out has me smiling and sliding my hands under her sweater, planting them just above her hips. "Not sick of me yet?" she asks.

"Never," I reply in a serious tone. I'm not sure she's ready to know just how much I'll never get sick of her.

"Maybe you can stay another night? At least until the sun is up. Maybe until the sun goes down and comes up again." Her smile has me weak enough to agree right away. I wish I could.

"I'd love to. You know that. I need fresh clothes. I need to get home and check on Crunch. I know my neighbors have been keeping an eye on him, but I want to see him for myself and know he's okay. And I'd love to stay all day and night, but I can't. I should check in at work. Haven't heard anything about the office being closed today. I could come back, but it'd be really late. I promised my brother and some friends that I'd watch the game with them at Orville's. It's our favorite bar in Syracuse. Actually, we have the whole weekend planned for Orville's. I can't be the ass that cancels on them." Then I add, "I'm sorry, Marce. This was all planned before we met. And Orville's opens no matter the weather or how much snow just got dumped."

She starts to pull away, letting her arms drop to her sides instead of keeping them around me. I try to hold on, but she puts her hands on my chest, literally pushing me away from her.

"No, no, no," I say, my hands up to her in submission. "Please don't do that. Don't pull back from me again. I will make time for you this weekend. I promise."

Marcy doesn't speak.

"You are far more important to me than any game. I just can't cancel on them. It wouldn't be fair."

But it's too late. Marcy's already shrinking away. I have no idea why.

"Marce, I'm going to need you to talk to me now. *Please*. Tell me what is going on. What is this?"

She merely shakes her head. "It's not you. It can't be."

## *Chapter 13*

*Marcy*

"IT CAN'T BE YOU," I tell Alec, not explaining what exactly this means. This major sports fan *can't* be my dream guy. I refuse to accept it. I promised myself that I'd never date anyone who liked sports again. I *promised*, and I have kept that promise all this time. The game would always win over me, no matter what game it is or where it is or what freaking team. I'd. Always. Lose.

"We're far too dissimilar," I add, instantly regretting my word choice. It's too easy to misinterpret or mishear. "We are too *different*. Nothing good can come of that."

"How can you possibly say that?" Alec pushes.

I carry on with my previous thread. It's the only thing I can do to hold myself together. "We are opposites, Alec."

"And people who have different interests can't possibly be a good couple together, right?" But his tone tells me he doesn't expect me to agree with this any more than he does.

"Yes, actually." I'm about to snap. Not at Alec, but within myself. I can't believe I fell for this kind of guy again. I can't believe that when Alec asked what it would take to fall in love with him, I was more than tempted to tell him it had already begun.

"How can the fact that I like to watch sports make you run in the other direction?"

I turn my eyes away from him, hoping this will get me out of having to answer. But because I can't help myself, I look back at him again anyway.

"How can an enjoyment of sports mean the end of us? Make this make sense to me, because I don't get it. I'll never get it, Marce. What is going on? How are you mad about my hobby?"

In a huff, I rush over to my little table by my sweet, little cocoon, wishing I could be wrapped in its safe warmth right now. Actually, I wish I could be wrapped up in the safe warmth of Alec right now. He held me in his arms only a few hours ago, cradling my body into his in my bed. The heat was already on. We didn't need each other for that. We each *wanted* the other close.

"This is the kind of man for me. The one I want." That was hard to choke out. Alec is the one I honestly want but can't have. "The one who crams months before his exams. The one who attends tech conferences. The one who excels in college and volunteers with charities. The one who travels the world to stay at the best hotels, not covered by a tiny piece of cloth in the woods." I shove the journal at him.

He takes it, his beautiful emerald eyes tiny slits as he glares at me. I point at what he holds. At my urging, he finally looks at the book in his hand. He starts to flip through. I swear it looks like he's about to fall over—literally—but then he kind of laughs.

Now I want to ask him what's going on.

His laugh practically echoes in my bedroom. It isn't long before he's serious again. No more than a few moments. "Are you kidding me with this?" he asks, looking back and forth between several pages the woman journaled on.

I shake my head no. There's no way I could form words without also forming tears, and perhaps a few sobs, so I refrain.

"You read these personal things." This is not a question.

I ignore this because, truthfully, that's the other worst thing about this whole situation. No matter how this book came into my possession, I still chose to read someone else's words about their life and their loved ones. My throat constricts, but not so much that I can't force out my next words. I almost wish it had. I wish I could make my stupid brain make my stupid mouth shut up. "Wick is the kind of man for me."

Alec's brows are scrunched. His entire face is, like every part is clamoring to get as close to his nose as possible. "You'd rather have a fictional guy?"

"He's real. I didn't know there was writing in this book when I bought it. Truly. I assumed it was brand new because it was in a bookstore that only sold new books. But this man, this son she talks about . . . I like him. I want him, or someone similar to him. Wick's . . . different from you."

"How so?" There is an unmistakable, sharp edge to his voice.

I continue, ignoring the voice in my head telling me to shut the hell up and let Alec help me out of this situation. "This Wick, he's, well, he's well-read, and kind, and intellectual."

"I'm not any of those things?" Apparently, it's Alec's turn to snap.

"You are. Of course you are. But all you seem to focus on is sports."

"And you. I focus most of my time on you."

This is yet another thing I ignore. Alec reads a few more entries. I'm sure he's already perused all of them at least twice based on how many times he's scanned the pages.

"Wick is perfect," I say, summoning up an attitude that I hope is enough to make Alec turn and leave. Or maybe push back. I'm so conflicted right now. Alec is also perfect. *Except for one thing . . .*

Alec keeps reading.

"Wick doesn't like sports," I add. *Just like me*, I could say, though that wouldn't be entirely true. I don't like sports for a very specific reason.

"How do you know?"

"Because." I huff, then quickly remind myself to rein this in. I'm trying to protect myself, not destroy Alec in the process. *Please don't let this hurt him.* "Not once does this woman mention Wick attending a game or playing sports of any kind."

"Where did you get this?" His voice is rough.

"I bought it at a bookstore in Syracuse. Why?"

Yet again, he flips through the pages, then gives a laugh. I fail to see what's so funny about this. "It must have gotten mixed up with things she returned," he says. "She probably forgot all about it. Can't tell it's been used from the look of the outside, or even flipping through casually." Which he then does for the twentieth time. "She'd be so amused to see this again, that's for sure. She'd most likely laugh her ass off."

It's my voice's turn to be rough and jagged. "What are you talking about?"

Alec finally glances up. It's the first time we've made eye contact since I shoved the book at him.

"This is my mom's book."

And just like that, all the air has left my lungs.

"This is our life," Alec continues, clearly unaware that the only reason I'm still standing right now is the fact that I leaned back against the side of my cocoon chair. But I just felt a wobble behind me, so it won't be long before I'm on the floor anyway. "I don't understand."

"You think I do? But I swear, this is my mom's book. It's her handwriting. It's us. We did all these things back then. NN is my name for my brother, like En-en for Henry. Wick is his name for me since he couldn't say my name either."

My body is completely still. Not a thing moves.

Alec pulls his phone out of his pocket, spends a few moments tapping and scrolling on the screen, then hands it to me. "Here."

"What is this?" My voice sounds really far away. I'm looking at the screen, but I'm not sure what I'm seeing.

"A text thread with my mom. Read it."

I force myself to move my eyes to Alec's face, then back down. As I scroll, he adds in an icy tone, "Before you suggest that I somehow found this stupid book and copied it, check the dates. Those texts go back weeks and months and years. An entire lifetime of nicknames."

I see the texts. I read each mention of Wick in Alec's phone, as far back as September of last year. I almost don't want to believe it. Then it clicks. The baby-talk pronunciation. *En-en* for *Henry* or *Hen-wee*, as a child would pronounce it. *Wick* like *A-wick*. I get it. "Oh my gosh." My body has roared back to life. My lungs suck breaths in and out at an alarming rate. My hearts pounds around to make up for lost time. The rest of me trembles. Alec is Wick. Wick is Alec. They are both one man: my perfect guy.

"Yeah. You want to ditch me for me." Alec gives me a hard glare.

"That's not what's happening here."

"Oh really? Do explain."

I can't actually *explain*, but I can put more of my side of things out there. At least, this is what I tell myself. "You don't share that version of you." I motion once again to the journal, though the more I highlight it, the more I see Alec flinch. "You tell me about ice hockey and naming your cat after a team and watching games with your brother, not when you went to Seattle or Munich or Tokyo or all the computer conventions you've gone to."

"I don't really think about that time much anymore. I was still in college then, trying to figure out my path in life. I was lost, thinking I wanted anything and everything and nothing. I know who and what I am now. You know what else I like? Camping. Know why?

Camping trips are usually the only moments my best friend actually opens up to me on how he feels about stuff. He tends to shut down real emotions. Shut me and our good friends out. He's spent so much time being a jackass and supposedly proud of that, but I know—and knew—better. Pete feels like he can be himself sitting around a campfire or fishing in the lake. It's at least easier to admit the shit he's going through then. The same goes for me. There's no judgment at the lake."

"Oh." There is no way I can say more. I wouldn't even know where to start. *I'm sorry* sounds so pitiful now, like it would only rub salt in Alec's emotional wound. The one I caused.

"Yeah."

I release a heavy breath. "Guess I'm a jackass. On two accounts. That." I motion to the book. "And the camping you do with Pete."

"I wouldn't call you a jackass," Alec replies, his voice softer than it's been in what feels like hours.

I don't deserve his kindness. I don't deserve for him to still care so much, as far as I can tell by his tone and his eyes. They are softer than they've been since the moment I told him I was more interested in another man. "No, but you might think it. You might be thinking it right now."

He doesn't say anything.

So maybe I'm wrong. Guess he really doesn't care anymore. Every look from him, every change in his voice, every flinch, pulls at my heartstrings, snaking them around into a massive twist of love, lust, concern, and regret.

I did this.

I ruined Alec.

I ruined us.

I can't handle any more. I can't carry on with my pathetic excuses for not wanting to be with this amazing man. Sports or no sports. I have to be brave, right? Dipshit Dane doesn't get to win again. "I'm so sorry, Alec. Really, I am. Do you think maybe we can just—"

"What? Pretend you weren't going to blow me off for some guy you never met—except, turns out you had? Turns out you've been screwing him for the past two days."

"That's not what this is or was."

"Sure as hell looks like it to me. Did you care about me at all? Or have any interest in me? If Wick is your dream guy, then why the hell bother with me?"

"Alec, I can explain." Only I can't. I know I'm not saying the right words to him.

He shakes his head, brushing my words away. "I'm nothing more than a dumb jock to you. Clearly."

I can't say that's not true because that's exactly how I've been treating him. I forced myself to think of him in those terms because it was easier than seeing him as a whole. He couldn't hurt me when he left if he was a dumb sports guy and *only* that.

Alec moves to set the book on the table, then straightens. He uses his empty hands to pull out and open his wallet, his eyes focused on the back of the book. For the price sticker, it suddenly occurs to me. He tosses a twenty on the table and, without so much as glancing my way, tells me, "That should cover it. I'm taking this." He motions with the book in his hand once again, and off he goes. Out of my life in the middle of the night.

I can't seem to stop him. Can't talk, can't move.

Can't bear the constant voice in my head screaming at me that this is all my fault. I crumble into my cocoon, hoping it'll swallow me whole and turn me into goo just like real caterpillars. Though I suspect there is no beautiful butterfly that will emerge from my chair. Just a broken, heart-smashed, tear-stained mess.

# Chapter 14

## Alec

I GLARE AT THAT freaking book sitting on my passenger seat practically the whole drive back to Syracuse. I don't care if the sun isn't up yet, and I don't care if Marcy wanted me to take the book or not. I don't even want it, and I'm sure my mom won't remember it. That's probably how it accidentally got returned to that store in the first place. No idea when or the logistics of any of it. Trying to figure it out hurts my brain.

Trying to figure out how Marcy could possibly have fallen for the me in that book but not the me who's been with her this whole time hurts my heart more.

At home, I take the book in with me. I can't leave it in my car. I also can't just chuck it into the trash like the sensible part of my brain tells me to. That damn book should mean nothing.

No, wait.

It *should* mean the end of me and Marcy.

She wanted a fantasy of sorts. She wanted a guy she didn't think she even knew. It shouldn't matter that that guy turned out to be me.

And yet.

I can't stop staring at that journal.

Mom wrote in there, yes. But I believe Marcy did, too.

That's what my brain won't shut up about. Did Marcy write about me? The me she spent all that time with? The me who took care of her? The one who's been falling in love with her? Was I ever on her mind? Or was it only about the me of years ago for her?

I storm over to where I tossed the book on my kitchen counter when I first came home, the full bottle of beer I'd grabbed and opened still in my right hand. After setting the beer down, I flip until I find the pages in the back where Mom wrote about me and Henry. I remember most of these stories. The little anecdotes of Mom's thoughts are somewhat new, for a few of them anyway. Mom isn't often shy about expressing what she feels to us.

Soon, though, my hands flip to the pages in the front. I know that if Marcy just got this book, and it's still only January, then that's where her entries would be. I should stop myself, but I don't. When I find handwriting different from my mom's, I pause on the page.

Marcy's writing starts the day we met.

She liked me from the beginning. That's obvious. My cheeks honestly burn reading what she thought of me. Other parts of me grow warm as well, but I tell them to back down and shut the hell up. That time is over now. We have reading to do. Then I see words I'm not sure what to do with. Also from the day we met.

*If I do get more of him, what happens if—or when—I have to let him go?*

What does that mean?

Why was she thinking about letting me go before things even really began?

I read on, finding out she thinks I'm cute when I'm nervous. This actually makes me laugh out loud because I'd been so awkward around her, I feared at one point that maybe she took pity on me for it. Nope. Turns out that was a turn-on for her. Guess not everything was pretend with her, like I've been convincing myself it had to be if she didn't really want me. But turning her on physically while not reaching the rest of her—like her *heart*—doesn't make me feel any better. Before all this, I dated, but never seriously. I didn't lie about not having had sex in a long time. I was waiting to find a woman worth giving more to. Then I met Marcy, and I thought she'd be the one to reach girlfriend level right away.

I skip over the first time she ended things with me. Not sure I'm in the right mindset to read that. Instead, I move on to Tuesday, the day the snowstorm began. I hadn't realized she'd taken a few moments to write. Must have been when I was asleep, as I was with her the whole rest of the time. To tell the truth, I'm shocked that she wasn't negative in her thoughts. She hurt both her ankle and her hip running away from me, and in between then, she couldn't decide whether she really wanted me to stay or go, not to mention all the panic she felt. Instead, she wrote things like:

*Alec was so patient with me, through all of it. If there was ever a perfect man for me, I'd be more than tempted to say it's him. But it's far too soon. Right? I wish there was someone I could honestly ask this question. Can Alec be my dream guy? Is he? More and more, it feels like the answer is an astounding* yes.

So what does *that* mean, then? What do I do with that?

Then there's this from yesterday:

*How can a man I've known for less than one week fit so perfectly into my life? And into my world, my apartment, even my bed. How can I like him this much? How can he mean so much to me already?*

I should stop. That's the recurring thought I have now. I shouldn't keep reading Marcy's personal notes, even if they are about me. But then, isn't that kind of how all this started? She read my mom's notes about me.

I have to go back to the beginning. Or at least to the beginning of the end. I have to know why she was afraid from the outset that she'd have to let me go. I flip back to the day she first walked out on me. She wrote so much, she took up the entire five-year page for it.

*I'm not sporty enough for Alec. That was made abundantly clear tonight. I thought he was joking at first, but then he said our potential ice-skating date could have turned into hockey. HOCKEY. As if I didn't hate it before, I hate it even more now that he didn't talk about himself on our first date. I babbled on and on about me, and all the while, he was hiding this secret side of him. Well, secret from me anyway. I'll never be the sporty girlfriend he expects me to be. I can never make him happy. He'll want to include me in things that I just have zero talent for or an abundant lack of skill. I'll have to choose between trying and embarrassing the hell out of myself, but more especially him—in FRONT OF HIS FRIENDS, no less—or pulling away, leaving Alec hurt and confused. I can't bear to hurt him. If only there was another side to him I don't know about. If only he chose to talk more about himself and let me in on what else makes him happy. But what if that's it? He likes sports. That is probably enough for him. It was all Dane ever wanted, and we all know Dane was never going to choose me over any hint of sporty anything. He dropped me far too many times. Abandoned from the beginning, and I should have seen it coming. I can't give Alec the chance to do that to me. I won't.*

Then I notice the Jane Austen quote on this page, from *Emma*. *If I loved you less, I might be able to talk about it more.*

It's official.

I'm an ass.

Marcy's words have me slowly lowering myself to one of the dining chairs, cradling the journal in my hands. She's scared. It's exactly like she said. She thinks I'll hurt her, or she'll hurt me, and it's all because her sports-obsessed dipshit ex flaked on her one too many times, apparently.

Then I get a new surge of anger and toss the book back down. It flutters closed.

I understand her fears, or at least that she has them. We could absolutely work through them together if she's willing, but for now, it's her turn to apologize. She and I can't move forward without that. If there's no regret on her side, everything means nothing, and it's time to move on alone.

·♥·♥·♥·♥·♥·

I wait two days before taking the journal to Mom.

Mom, of course, is happy to see me despite the fact that I never told her ahead of time to expect me. I didn't jump right into the reason for my visit either. But now that we're sitting here in the living room and I have the journal in my hands, I wish I'd done this over the phone. That would have made it easier to hide my feelings about the whole thing and be more stoic about it all. I know that's definitely not going to happen now.

Somehow, I manage to tell Mom the story of Marcy finding this journal at the bookstore and where it has led. Well, I leave out the part where Marcy decided she liked book me over real me.

Mom laughs like I originally did. She doesn't grow serious like I did, however.

"How does this not bother you?" I ask. "Isn't it like the equivalent of Marcy reading your diary?"

"Oh, I don't know. It clearly slipped my mind that I ever used it or parted with it. If I'd found it or bought it without knowing, I'm sure I'd read it, too." Then she looks up at me. She doesn't say anything right away. Just lets me wonder what's going on, which is unusual for her. Mom only does this when she wants Henry or me to figure something out for ourselves.

Mom picks up the journal and flips to the pages she wrote on. She gives a few small smiles at the memories, then she flips to the front.

"What are you doing?" I ask, my voice tight, but it's too late.

Mom finds Marcy's entries.

I lean forward and reach across the coffee table for the book, but Mom's already skimmed at least half of Marcy's pages as she flipped quickly through before I try to pluck it out of her hands. Mom refuses to let go. So do I.

"I hadn't realized she used it, too."

"Yeah. She also decided she likes book me more than real me," I admit reluctantly. I can't bear to say more. I haven't moved from my new spot either. All I can do is grip the open journal and fight every single urge I have to lean in more and admire Marcy's handwriting again. But doing so would force me to read about her fears and her insecurities, and the lump in my throat tells me I cannot handle that right now.

"Wick, your name is on every page Marcy used."

I shrug in reply.

Mom's eyes lift and bore into me. She finally loosens her grip on the book so I can take it. I straighten as she tells me, "Don't you dare stand there and act like that means nothing. You saw what happened between your dad and I when he shut down like that."

"Marcy and I aren't married. We aren't even dating."

Mom motions with the journal. "Could have fooled me, son."

I amend my answer. "Anymore."

"Did you read what she wrote?"

"Yeah. She doesn't want me."

"No, Wick." Mom shakes her head. "Not even close. She's scared. Terrified that you are going to destroy her like this Dane guy did."

I hate even hearing my mom say that asshole's name. I also hate that I can't admit how I really feel. Mom never holds back on me. I don't want to hold back, but my anger at Marcy keeps getting the best of me. "That doesn't matter. Marcy used her history with someone else against me. She also wanted to leave me for a guy she didn't know. It doesn't matter that that guy turned out to be me." *I deserve an apology.*

"Really?" It's been a long time since I heard such frustration and disappointment in Mom's voice. "If you don't understand—genuinely *understand*—what I'm saying right now, then no, it doesn't matter. But if you see the importance of your name all over this journal, *Marcy's* journal—because it *is* hers now—then you know what you need to do."

"She didn't even sound sorry for it." *Except she did.* I can almost hear her sweet voice. *I'm so sorry, Alec. Really, I am. Do you think maybe we can just—*

And I'd cut her off. I didn't let her finish whatever she was going to say. I went on the offensive in true "hurt or be hurt" style.

"You had a good childhood growing up."

I nod in agreement and give Mom a small smile. "The best."

"There's never been any trauma you've had to deal with."

There hasn't, and thank God for that.

"Did you ever have any toxic dating relationships?"

"Not really. Dating was just dating. Nothing serious. Nothing I ever got hurt over."

Mom takes in a breath, then motions for me to sit again. I do. "Wick, intellectually, you might be able to understand trauma, but there's no way to really know what happened to Marcy and how hard it was for her unless and until you ask her. This Dane guy clearly did a number on her."

"Can we stop saying his name?" I ask, rubbing my temple. "It's bad enough thinking about him ever having been loved by Marcy. It helps when she calls him Dipshit Dane instead of just his first name."

Mom laughs. "I noticed that in the journal." She grows serious again. "'Abandoned.'"

"What?"

"That's the word Marcy used. That dipshit abandoned her, more than once. Why did she say you kept secrets from her?"

While still holding the journal, I put my hands up. "I never kept secrets from her."

"But you weren't an open book. You weren't forthcoming with what makes you *you*. Why?"

I shift in my seat. It almost feels like I'm squirming. And yeah, I think I am. I'm beginning to wilt under Mom's questioning. She's asking things I should have asked myself. "I liked hearing about her. I wanted to know everything there is to know about her."

"You feel like you do?"

"Well, I thought so. Now, I'm not sure. She told me Dipshit was an ass and that he broke her heart, but she never explained how or why. I just assumed it was a typical breakup."

Mom lets out a breath, then shakes her head. "Sweetheart, there is no such thing as a 'typical' breakup. In some ways, I'm glad that your heart hasn't gotten broken like that." She pauses. "Or has it?"

"Before Friday, I would say no. Now . . . yeah, I think it has," I finally admit. It feels good to let that out.

"Well, breakups are hard. Having someone stomp on your fragile heart, then walk away? That's soul-crushing. I experienced this from your dad. I know he's a decent guy, but he didn't want to be married to me. He didn't want to put in even a single ounce of effort to actually feel married to me and live a life like spouses do. I don't mean living together or having sex."

"Gross," I add with a scrunched face, just to relieve some of the tension of this topic.

Mom laughs dutifully, but sobers quickly. "I just mean your dad wasn't available emotionally. We never connected. He abandoned me." Mom takes a moment to sip her water.

I know she used that word for a reason. It applies to both her and Marcy.

"So again I say, if you know how much you really do mean to Marcy, you know what you need to do."

## *Chapter 15*

*Marcy*

"Marce, stop being a baby and realize this will only help you," Cass says.

"No way. Uh-uh. I am *not* telling Lourdes my stupid, pathetic, brokenhearted—or whatever the hell this is—story," I explain to Yvonne and Cass on our lunch break.

Another worker is covering the front for Yvonne, and Cass can design whenever the mood strikes. I've been busy in the office working on social media and the website. Apparently, I'm not "chipper" enough to work with customers right now. I've also been accused of "slacking" on my job, even when stuck alone in the office. Not by Lourdes. But Yvonne and the other workers who run the front, as well as several customers I had the misfortune of running into that first day after Alec was gone, haven't held back.

I can't help that I'm also stuck creatively. Despite my nonchalance to my friends slash coworkers, I *am* brokenhearted. It would mortify me for Lourdes to know the cause of this. I absolutely prefer her to think I'm just floundering for no reason.

"I don't think she's being a baby," Yvonne tells Cass. "She's obviously afraid of something."

"Yeah, of Lourdes using her psychological superpowers to suss me out and get me to spill my emotional guts," I say, laughing and attempting to make light of the situation.

Neither Cass nor Yvonne laugh in return.

"It's been a week," Yvonne says gently. "He hasn't contacted you this entire week?"

I avoid eye contact. "He has. He's texted me often since Sunday."

"Way to hold back important information," Cass tells me. She gives an almost-chuckle, like she can't believe I'm being this difficult. I've had conversations like this with her before, so it's a fair assumption.

"Let me guess: you're ignoring him again. Just like you did last time you ran away from him."

I put a hand up. "Hey. He ran this time."

Cass looks like she's trying not to roll her eyes. Her right eye even twitched. "No, he left because you made him. You pushed him away. You told him you wanted someone else. Who's actually him. It's no wonder he didn't take it well."

With this, I heave a sigh. "I know." I draw out that last word. "It's my fault. I freaked out. I ran him off. I *hurt* him, and I never meant to. I was just so scared of him hurting me." And now my vision is blurry once again as my eyes tear up.

Pretty soon, it's time to return to work. Well, they both say it is, but then I notice Lourdes lingering nearby, leaning against the doorjamb of the office, where Yvonne, Cass, and I have been eating our food.

Shit.

I adore Lourdes, but I really don't want to be alone with her right now. I can see her analytical eyes scrutinizing my face. When the other two leave the room, she steps in and shuts the door. After a few moments more silently watching me, she speaks.

"I won't demand it, and you don't have to tell me anything, but I know what a broken heart feels like. Mine was trampled on almost ten years ago, and I've never really recovered. While a lot of people know what happened, most don't know how not over it I am. I never mention that part."

"I get that," I say with a sigh. I understand it far more than I'd like to. My eyes start to burn.

"I'm sorry that you know how this feels. What Spence did . . . I really hope your guy did nothing of the same or even close to it. But if he's as good a man as Spence was before all that went down, I know that sometimes, letting go isn't always the right answer, depending on the situation. Even then, I still love Spence, and only two other people in the world know that."

She means her besties Gwenn—who I have much more admiration for after experiencing my own snowed-in love affair—and Lucy—who's Alec's best friend's girlfriend.

I didn't let my tears fall during my entire conversation with my two work friends, yet one confession from my boss, and I'm suddenly turning into a weeping mess. It's far too much to hold in. I tell her everything that happened with Alec and me, including my short obsession with Wick. I even tell Lourdes the sordid details of what really happened with me and Dipshit Dane, things she never knew before.

"Oh wow." Her voice is soft. It takes her forever to speak again. "That's a tricky one," she adds. She doesn't call me crazy or laugh in my face like I expected her to. She's honestly the only one who knows the whole truth. I only told Yvonne and Cass that Alec and I stopped dating and how hard I'm taking it, not the circumstances of why.

Meanwhile, I am a blubbering heap of tears. "I know. I'm so stupid. I focused so much on Alec's affinity for the outdoors and for sports that I ignored the amazing parts of him, like his intelligence, how much he understood the technical aspects of my job, how kind and loving he is—" I choke on that word. *Loving.*

This gets Lourdes's attention. "If you really don't want to answer this question, we can both pretend it never happened, but I think this is something you need to hear."

"What's that?"

She pauses a moment. "Was Alec loving or in love?"

I immediately shake my head at her. "It's crazy to fall in love so soon." I know this isn't a direct answer to her question. I also know that I'm already there. Possibly by the time he had to help me hobble up to my apartment. Definitely by the time he left it. And all I did was push him away, time and time again. It doesn't feel like I deserve those few glorious days we had together in the middle of all that.

"Maybe," she says in reply. "Who's to say? There is no specific timeline to follow. I was in love with Spence as a teenager, before we ever dated. There are couples who fall in love and marry within months of meeting each other. If that doesn't feel right for you, okay. But if you really do love him and you're just scared, remember that Alec sure as hell isn't Dipshit Dane. He won't abandon you on the side of the road to attend a game that isn't even happening until the next damn day."

"How do you know that?" I ask in a whisper. Lourdes has hit me right to my core. She brought up the fear I can't stop thinking about. The one that's been on my mind since Alec and I met.

"How do you not?" Lourdes replies.

I stay quiet. Truth is, I do know that Alec would never. I've known it since he was determined for me to know the truth about him not actually having a girlfriend, even if his way of getting to it was awkward.

"I know it the same way you do," Lourdes continues. "He cared for you at a time that it would have been easy to leave. When he first took you to your apartment, the snow wasn't that bad. It only worsened the longer he stayed there. Hell, Alec worked on your car here long before taking you home. Dipshit Dane would have given up and left. In fact, he probably never would have shown up in the first place. I know men like him. And while Alec couldn't take off once the snow and the blackout made leaving impossible, he didn't have to stay that Thursday when the all clear was given. He didn't ask for anything in return."

"How happy are Gwenn and Rhett?" I ask suddenly.

Lourdes smiles like she understands exactly what I'm getting at. "The happiest." Then she adds, "Is Alec a grand gesture kind of guy?"

"I think in this instance, a deep, heartfelt apology is what he needs."

# Chapter 16

## Marcy

CALLING OR TEXTING ALEC would be smartest, just to make sure he's home, but I'm full of too many questions for that. What if he gets mad? Or hangs up on me? What if he doesn't even answer? It's been one week since we've seen each other. One week since we've connected in any way. A week of me ignoring every single attempt of his to reconnect.

Of course, my plan isn't foolproof. There are still options he has that don't involve actually listening to me or acknowledging me, but I'm willing to take the risk.

When it's late enough in the evening that I think it's safe to assume he's home from work, I drive out to Syracuse and over to Alec's apartment. He's there. The lights shining through the curtains give me hope.

After knocking on the door, I'm not sure what to do with my hands.

Jamming them into my pockets feels strange.

Holding on to and twisting my hair makes me feel thirteen again.

Finally, I hold them together, interlacing my fingers.

Alec hasn't answered yet.

I'm about to lean closer and knock on the door again when it swings open. He's still in a suit from work, though his jacket, tie, and socks are missing. "Marce?"

I should take it as a good sign that he's using his nickname for me. This should propel my thoughts forward. Instead, I go with the most off-the-wall thing I can think of. "My neighbors found the ham they thought their dog ate."

"O-kay." This is said slowly, both syllables emphasized.

"Also, I found the button I accidentally ripped off your dress shirt. It was under my nightstand after all."

"You couldn't text me with that? Or with *anything*?" Alec asks, his facial features still bunched up together.

This was a terrible idea. Of course it was. I came up with it. I shake my head. "Yes, you're right. I could have. I should have." But I'm just stupid and daring and masochistic enough to follow this with, "Can I come in?"

Alec eyes me, wary, but then he steps aside and opens the door fully. Then he quietly shuts the door behind me and moves a few feet away from the foyer area. I'm on the floor mat in front of the door. Not speaking. Everything is still in my head.

*It's not about you. It's about Dane.*

*He hurt me. He destroyed me. By choice.*

*I unfairly projected that onto you. I blamed you. I compared you to him. You are nothing like him. You are the best man I've ever met.*

*I'm so, so sorry.*

*Please forgive me.*

*I think I'm in love with you.*

When Alec first came to the floral shop, he was adorably awkward and out of place. I was the confident one, saying all the right things. I'm saying all the right things now, except they're all in my head and won't come out of my mouth. Nothing will  Still, Alec watches me. He doesn't speak. Doesn't try to help me out in any way with prompts or words of his own.

I spin on the balls of my feet—not an easy thing to do in winter boots—and hightail it out of his place, rushing to the door, then slamming it behind me on my way out. I shove my glove-less hands into my pockets, finding Alec's button in the left one. Alec doesn't call me back.

It's official. I blew it. I panicked and ruined what should have been the perfect apology. I couldn't him all the things I planned to say. Not even a squeaky, little *"sorry"* came out.

There's no way he will forgive me now. That was my chance. I'm guessing my very last one. Alec must still be angry with me about Wick or about not answering his texts—which, let's be honest, all only said that we needed to talk but nothing more—because I've never seen him so broodingly silent like that. If he ever tires of mortgages, he'd be a shoo-in for any part in a historical drama.

I get in my car and start the drive back to the Falls, and still—*still*—nothing from Alec.

# Chapter 17

## Alec

MARCY JUST LEFT.

I mean, she just *left*.

What the hell was that?

I've been texting her for days, telling her we need to talk. I didn't want to say everything in text messages and voicemails, so I left it at that. She ignored every single plea. Then she showed up here, and I became Nervous Alec again. I couldn't form anything cohesive enough to say out loud.

I stare at the door long after she's gone.

Then a thought occurs to me. It's neither slow nor gradual. I know why she was here. After who only knows how much time has passed since she suddenly showed up at my front door until now, I figure it out. She wanted to apologize. Her face said so. So did her eyes. I hadn't realized this when she was in front of me. The only thoughts that were in my brain with her in front of me again after the cluster that was our last interaction were of sweeping her into my arms, kissing her, telling her to forget everything I said—all my anger and shock, all of it—and begging her to start over with me. We deserve that with each other. We deserve to be happy together.

Though I'm well aware it's far too late, I lunge toward the door and yank it open, searching for any sign of her. But again, she's long gone. There's no way she hung around after my silent staring. She must have taken that to mean refusal or rejection. I meant neither of those things.

Slowly, I close the door again. Somehow, I find myself dropping down to my sofa. After I called Marcy following my talk with Mom and Marcy subsequently ignored me, I was one hundred percent certain that I was right the first time and Mom was wrong. Of course, it probably would have been the one and only instance of this.

The urge I feel right now is to follow Marcy back to her place and talk things out, maybe kiss things out after, but that can't be good to chase her down, I don't think. I'm not entirely sure. I need someone else to talk to about this. A second opinion of sorts. Henry would be a good option, apart from the fact that he's now in Florida with Effie. I can't interrupt their vacation for my relationship melodrama.

While he is my best friend, Pete and I have never really discussed relationships like this, apart from his with Lucy. They're in a weird place right now, though. Some serious relationship issues there. I can't add mine to his misery.

But thinking of Pete and Lucy reminds me that there is actually someone who could help.

This is probably the worst idea I've ever had, while potentially still the best. The worst best? I'm going through with it anyway.

·♥·♥·♥·♥·♥·

"This is Lourdes." Her words are clipped, her tone stony. Or maybe it's just neutral and I haven't been able to get a read on her yet.

Once again, I'm afraid tracking down her personal phone number was not the best idea. Reluctantly, I initially sidestepped Pete and Lucy, knowing they are struggling with each other. But calling the flower shop and trying to convince Marcy's coworkers to help me didn't go well. It took me two days to get the right information. Two days of pleading with people who probably already know Marcy's side of things.

How many of them let me go on and on about how important this was with no intention of helping just to screw with me? And the number of them who told me they simply don't trust me . . . I'm sure I deserved that, but it sucked all the same. Finally, I broke down and asked Pete, who silently handed over Lucy's number. I expected a lecture from her, but she was pretty quiet about the whole situation, too. However, that doesn't mean she didn't bias Lourdes against me, in addition to whatever Marcy told her boss.

I feel like it's been forever to get through all this. It's now Monday, three days since Marcy showed up at my apartment.

"Hi. This is Alec. I've been dating Marcy. Well, I *was* dating Marcy. I'm the one who got trapped in the snowstorm with her. The one from the journal."

"I know who you are," Lourdes tells me. She doesn't say more.

Not sure if that's a bad sign or not, but I keep going. "Marcy isn't speaking to me right now."

"I know this, too."

"She's scared. She thinks our differences should keep us apart. She's afraid that I'll end up using those differences against her like I'm assuming her asshole of an ex did."

"She came to see you."

"Yeah. She did. She showed up at my place the other night," I say. "It was weird. Not Marcy. Never Marcy. She's, well, she's perfect. But the way she acted was odd. I think she was there to apologize, but I hadn't realized that at the time. I was too shocked that she was even there. I wanted to take her in my arms and kiss her, but I didn't want to spook her. Only she didn't move or speak or anything, then she ran off. I don't need an apology from her."

"You don't?" For the first time, Lourdes's voice is far less neutral.

"I thought I did. And rightfully so."

Lourdes is silent. I can't tell whether this means she agrees with me.

"Look, I don't like that she clearly compared me to her asshole ex, and I don't like that she used the journal version of me against me. She didn't know that's what she was doing, and I didn't know about it at all. But in some ways, I think I understand now that the version of me from her journal can actually bring us together."

"She doesn't have the journal anymore. You took it."

"Technically, I bought it from her, but it is hers. I get that. And I think you can help me get it back to her."

"What would you like me to do?" This isn't asked with a bitchy or impatient tone. Rather, it's a kind one. I think this is going to work.

# Chapter 18

## Marcy

I AM NOT GOING to think about Alec.

These are the words I tell myself all day long.

*I am not going to think about Alec.*

I refuse to think about how his hair spills a little over his forehead after a shower because he never dries it enough. I also refuse to recall the way his strong, muscular arms held tight to me as we lay in my bed that last night of the winter storm, silently assuring me that I was safe with him. That's another thing I will not focus on. The fact that I had my perfect man, and it had nothing to do with the version of him on paper. I just stupidly didn't see this. It's Friday. One week since I ran from his apartment after epically failing to give him any sort of apology.

The recollection of this bitters the taste in my mouth, just moments before a pleasant sweetness from the cinnamon latte I've been sipping at my work area in Lourdes's office while I work on figuring out a small bug pestering the website.

"Hey, Marce?" Lourdes asks, popping her head around the open door. She doesn't bother moving the rest of her body to come in here. "Can you help me for a sec? I've got a massive last-minute delivery, and everyone else has left."

"Is it that late already?" I glance at the clock on my computer, then I remember that I removed it from the screen two hours ago, as the minutes mocked me, a constant reminder that I don't have anyone to meet at the end of the workday. I don't have the man I want most to wrap my arms around. I can't kiss him for an indefinite amount of time and complain about needing sleep for tomorrow's workday but still not leave for hours because I belong with him wherever he is. Despite every way I've looked at this, that is the truth. Our truth, Alec's and mine.

I never do deliveries, but I do sometimes pitch in to help load them. I assume that's what Lourdes is asking me for. She leads the way to the work area. I see in front of me that the *entire* work table is covered in clear vases full of red sweet peas and orange-yellow chrysanthemums.

"I added a few little extra things for flourish," Lourdes says next to me as I spot the daisies and leucadendron in each arrangement.

"What . . . but how . . . Alec?" I ask, though I know it was him. I hope. Is it too much to hope?

I see Lourdes nod out of the corner of my eye. I can't look directly at her. I can't tear my eyes from this magnificent spectacle of flowers.

"Oh." I should say more, I just don't have any other words.

*Alec.* I miss that man. I miss his voice whispering in my ear and his arms around me and his laugh. This . . . this is something I hadn't expected.

"He really is adorably clueless about flowers, but he remembered the ones you picked for his mom's flowers, and he also remembered the ones you said were your favorites."

I turn and look to see Lourdes staring at me, waiting for a response. "What?" I ask innocently.

She shakes her head, clearly knowing I'm trying to deflect. "You never tell anyone your favorite flowers. Just the ones we're trying to sell that day. You claim *those* are your favorites to any customer who asks. But you actually told Alec the truth, before you two ever had a date."

I don't reply. I can't form words, these stupid tears threatening to slip down out of my eyes. I blink furiously to make them go away, but it's no use.

Lourdes continues. "He ordered an entire table of flowers just for you. He took a risk and asked your boss—your *friend*—for help. He worked really hard just to get my number so he could ask me for help. Something to think about."

When I manage to look over at Lourdes after more furious blinking and sniffling, she gives me a smile. "Alec said you can take them all home, give them all away, keep them all here—which I'm okay with, too. Whatever you want. He just wants you to be happy. You already know he misses you." Then she walks into the small back room with the coolers, giving me time alone to think.

I pull out my phone and call Alec with shaky hands. Slowly, I let a breath out, waiting for him to answer. "What did you do?" I ask as soon as he answers. The tears refuse to be held in anymore.

"You okay, Marce?" he replies immediately.

My breath hitches as I cry a bit harder. I can't answer him.

"Hey, I'm sorry," Alec says. "I thought the flowers would make you happy. I didn't mean to push. I don't want you to feel pressured. I'm so sorry. I just—"

"No, I'm sorry. I went a little crazy. More than a little. I never should have read your mom's journal, even without knowing it was hers. I never should have compared you to anyone else. I am so, so sorry, and I will regret it every day."

"Marce, I should have—"

"It's okay," I interrupt him again. I hate interrupting people, but I can't let him think he's done something wrong or something I don't like. "I'm okay. These are happy tears."

"You mean that? They don't sound happy."

I give a small laugh and nod. Then I laugh again as I tell him I nodded as if he could see me, because I don't really have the words to say how I feel right now.

"Marce, I will read every romance and mystery and thriller and historical fiction you want me to. I'll learn all the computer programs and coding jargon that I don't already know, which honestly is more than you think. I know *so* much about computers. We really do have that in common. And we can work on the rest. We can stay at inns or hotels instead of in tents, and go visit art museums and bookstores, and only be outside just to get to and from the car. I'll go wherever you want and do whatever you want."

"Please don't change yourself for me," I tell him. I almost beg this of him.

Now Alec gives a small laugh. "I'm still going to be me. I'll still like sports and camping, and I'll continue to do those things. But I can be me and be with you, too. You wanted the dream guy from the book? I'm him. Literally."

I take a slow breath in and out.

"I'm not mad anymore," he adds. "And really, I think I was more hurt than anything. I was falling so hard for you, and you pulled the rug out from under me. But I get it. I know having differences scares you. One big difference in particular. One I share with a certain person who will remain nameless, though I admit I love the nickname you gave him."

He will absolutely remain nameless right now. I hope to never have to think of that guy ever again. "I'm sorry," I whisper.

"I know," Alec replies. "It's okay. I'm sorry, too. I . . . I read your journal entries."

"Wait. What?" This has everything slowing down just as it was all speeding up.

"At the time, I told myself I was doing it just because you read all of my mom's notes. It was a way to make it even. More than that, I just wanted to figure you out, I guess. I wanted to know if what I thought we'd had up to that point was real."

"It was. Of course it was." My voice is still soft. "It is."

"It is," he repeats, his smooth voice also a whisper. "My name is in every single one of your entries."

"It is," I echo. A smile tugs at the sides of my mouth. I hadn't badmouthed him in any way. Never wanted to. Every word I wrote about Alec was how much I was falling for him and how much it terrified me. I'm actually glad he knows all of that now without me having to say it out loud.

I take another slow breath in and out. "Are these flowers my Valentine's Day presents?" Valentine's Day is four days away.

He gives me another amazing laugh. "Nope. That one's still here with me."

"You have a present for me? What made you think you'd need it?"

"Hope." The laugh is no longer in his voice. "I hoped, Marcy. You tried scaring me away because you're scared. But I couldn't let go of my hope. I think you and I would be great together if you'd just give us a chance. The time we spent snowed in proves that."

He's right. Of course he is. I'm nodding again.

"You have to say something, or start a video chat," Lourdes says, her head peeking around the corner from the cooler.

I give her a laughing smile. "You off work?" I ask Alec.

"In five more minutes. Where would you like to meet?"

"Would it be worth it to you to come to my apartment even though it's supposed to snow? We might get trapped again."

"Marcy, I would go anywhere for you. And being secluded with you is far superior to anything else that I might do in a snowstorm. Wouldn't want to be anywhere else."

I smile to myself, but it's all for Alec. "See you in a few?"

"Be there as soon as I can."

Lourdes is grinning when I turn to her again. "Your grandma would like these, wouldn't she?" I nod to one of the vases. After all, Lourdes's grandma built this business from scratch. She's damn proud of the work Lourdes and all our team have put in to keep this shop one of the best in the area, at least when her dementia lets go enough for her to remember. With or without those precious memories, I know there is still so much attachment Mrs. Leggero-Shaye has for flowers and this life in general.

"Absolutely. She'll smile all day from them."

"What do you think about delivering these to our elderly residents in town? I'll keep one for me at home and one here, but I think it would be nice to share the rest."

Lourdes gives another grin. "I think we should totally do that. Tomorrow, although I will take one home for Gam-Gam tonight. She can have it next to her favorite chair in the living room. I swear it'll make her day. You enjoy your night with Alec. And Marce? It's okay to be scared. I'm terrified of the feelings I have for Spence, and . . . well, that isn't important. Just know that Alec isn't one to run. He isn't going to abandon you. I can tell. He isn't Dipshit Dane."

"I know that now. I wish I knew it before."

We lock up both doors and head to our respective homes. Thankfully, my vase of flowers stays upright as I navigate my way down the few roads to my apartment. Alec arrives a little while later. I let him in, and we seat ourselves on the sofa. Then he places the journal on my coffee table and quickly stands, carefully pulling me to my feet as well.

"Maybe we should start again." Alec nods. He holds out his right hand.

I give him mine, assuming he's just going to shake it. But he takes my hand in his like it's the most precious, tender, delicate thing he's ever held, and he doesn't let go. He doesn't break eye contact, either. "Hi, Marcy. My name is Alec Russell. My mom and brother call me Wick. It's a holdover from when my brother and I were little. I really like sports and camping and being outdoors. I also really like computers and technology and traveling. I made the dean's list in college, graduated with honors, and I work in mortgages now. I will never say no to a word game or puzzle."

"Hi, Alec." I give him a shy smile as he gently squeezes my hand. "My full name's Marcy Layla Haskens. I, too, really like computers and technology and traveling. I kind of hate the outdoors. My ex-boyfriend screwed with my head so much that I am extremely suspicious of anyone who likes sports. I'm working on this issue, and I'll do my best to keep it from interfering in future relationships. Or current ones," I add in a whisper, leaning closer to him conspiratorially. Then I straighten, my smile widening. "My favorite games are on the computer or a folding piece of cardboard. And I never was sure if I believed in love at first meeting until you came along."

"I changed your mind?"

I nod, starting to feel breathless.

"And now that I have?"

It's impossible to hold back a grin. It's also impossible to not touch this man any longer. I reach out, and he steps closer, our arms enfolding each other. "I'm no longer scared to ask you if I've had any affect on you, too."

Alec lowers and turns his head just a bit to kiss my temple before straightening back up. "Let me put it to you this way. I've known you for less than a month, and I can't imagine my life without you." He pauses. "I know so much about your life, who you are, and who you've been. You told me so many stories that I feel like I've known you forever. That's when I really started falling for you. That first date when you told me your life story."

"At your urging."

He laughs. "Yes, at my urging. I wanted to know everything about you. I didn't stop to think that maybe you needed that from me, too."

"I did."

Even though Alec in no way makes me nervous, admitting how deep my feelings are has me lightheaded and tingly. I need to ground myself a little before continuing this thread of conversation.

"I hope it's okay," I say, motioning to the vase of flowers, "but I'm only keeping two. The rest are going to some of our elderly neighbors. Just want to put that out there in case you weren't actually serious about me giving them away."

Alec moves forward, his arms tightening around my waist, his face so close, I feel his warm, minty breath on my skin. "I mean what I say, Marce, and I know how kind and giving you are. It's one of the many things I've discovered I love about you."

He could mean that in different ways. He loves things *about* me but not me specifically? He loves *me* and all my pieces? I have to know for sure. "You love me?"

# Chapter 19

## Alec

THERE'S NO SQUEAK IN her voice when Marcy asks if I love her. No shakiness, either. I think she's finally ready. "It's early," I start slowly. "I know that. I started developing these feelings much earlier than I expected. Falling in love doesn't follow some timeline, though."

Marcy nods, her eyes damp with burgeoning tears.

I see what she means about nodding to me while we were on the phone. "And while I still don't know about love at first sight, I definitely believe in love at first conversation. I learned a lot from you that day, before we ever made it to dinner."

"Within minutes of meeting you, I told you something I never tell anyone else."

For a few moments, as I slowly caress her back, I think about when we first met. Her sparkly eyes. Her pink cheeks. How kind and patient and helpful she was. "The flowers." It finally dawns on me. "You don't tell anyone your favorite flowers?"

She gives a quick head shake. "It feels too personal. But I told you."

Now my eyes sting with wetness. I try to blink it away. "You are the only woman I've been nervous around since college, when I had no confidence whatsoever. And it wasn't so much that I wasn't confident in your attraction to me. It was that I couldn't find the right words to say that I was taken by you from the start. I couldn't find words to say to you at all." I give her a laughing smile, recalling all my awkwardness. She moves closer, pressing her body fully against mine, as I add, "I have to ask, though. You don't know that much about me. My fault, absolutely. But how did you still fall for me? How are we here now? I know my reasons, but I don't know yours."

"No?" she asks, but her soft tone tells me maybe I know more than I think. "Your heart, Alec. I adore your heart. You braved a snowstorm to make sure I was okay. You rescued me from said snowstorm not once but twice. You were as patient as someone could be through all my panic. You took care of me in a way no one else has."

The pink in her cheeks deepens. She looks down a moment then back up to me. Her hands begin to stroke up and down the back of my neck. I gently tighten my hands on her hips, keeping her anchored to me.

"You were a total gentleman even when it was obvious you wanted more because you needed to know how I felt first. You never pushed. Even in the beginning, I knew you were different, in the very best way. I knew I wanted everything good you were willing to give me."

"Maybe there is something to the love at first sight concept." That last bit I say in a whisper.

I know something now. I'm going to marry this woman one day. It's not time for a proposal, but, after all we've been through this month, I think I'd marry her tomorrow if she asked.

We share a smile, then the sweetest kiss I could ever ask for from the most incredible woman I've ever known. Her lips are soft yet hungry for mine. I give her all I have. I'll always give her all I have, even as I pull her up to me. She wraps her legs around my waist, and I carry her to the sofa. When I lower us to sit down, she ends up straddling me.

Marcy pulls back for a breath, so I tip my face up and give her a gentle kiss on the forehead.

"I promise this," Marcy says. "I promise I'm never running from you again."

Now I lean my forehead against hers. "Good. I'm not sure how your body would take another slip in the snow."

She laughs for a moment. "And Alec?" Her voice quivers.

"Yeah?"

"Can I come to your next football party?"

My eyes are definitely teary now. I know for sure it's love if she's willing to do that. Not only willing but wanting. "You can come to any party you want."

"I love you," she whispers.

"I love you, too, Marce."

I'm just about to kiss her again when she quickly puts a hand on my cheek to gently stop me. "How annoying would it be if I asked you to teach me about the game while it's on? Or should I study beforehand?"

I plant the softest of kisses on her cheekbone, then one down on her jaw. "I'll study with you, if you want. I am an excellent test taker. I know all the tricks for remembering everything in a short amount of time."

She nods. "You are my intelligent, sporty, outdoorsy, world-traveling dream guy, and I wouldn't have it—or you—any other way."

MARCY AND ALEC'S STORY in Winter Blossoms actually takes place during the timeline of June Days. By the time Lourdes and Spence's story comes along, Alec and Marcy are a well-established couple.

Speaking of Lourdes, I adore her, her flower shop, and all her staff, especially Marcy. I wouldn't have any idea how a flower shop is run without the amazing help of Courtney Rapp at Westcott Florist in Syracuse, NY.

I also want to thank Sarah Kil for another fabulously stunning cover.

Thank you, Joanne Lui—the best editor ever! Your notes always make me smile, even when they result in a lot more work for me to do.

Special thank you to my friends and family for always cheering me on though you might not know what I'm working on, such as surprise projects like this one.

A down deep to my core, heartfelt thank you to my darling husband and sweet son for being so understanding about all the time it takes me to write these books and for knowing that when I'm hunkered down in writing mode, it won't last forever. I love you both.

Finally, thank you, reader, for returning again to Syracuse Falls. If this was your first time there, I do hope you'll visit again with the other characters and their stories.

# Bonus Epilogue

## Marcy

MY BOYFRIEND HAS COMPLETELY converted me to something I swore I'd always hate, and I'm not complaining one bit.

That's the conclusion I've come to. Never did I ever suspect I'd not only enjoy watching sports with him but also look forward to the games, whether on TV, online, or in person.

We're actually about to leave with plans to meet up with Alec's brother Henry and Henry's girlfriend Effie at our favorite local bar for lunch and a baseball game. I was running a little late on the way here from the Falls, so Alec tells me to transfer my overnight bag from my car to his instead of dropping it off inside his apartment.

"No sense taking extra time away," he tells me.

I answer with a shrug, though I'm not sure it matters either way. We're still a little behind where we should be. "You should call or text Henry and let him know we're on our way."

Alec gives me a liquefying smile. Those smiles of his melt just about everything on me. They always have, ever since the day he walked into the flower shop where I work and nervously fumbled his way through buying a bouquet for his mom and flirting with me.

"Already taken care of," he replies.

I grin at him in return. "Should be a good game today," I say as we climb into his car and fasten our seat belts.

Then I turn my body slightly and watch Alec guide the car down the road. Watching him is one of my favorite things to do. Only I notice that he turns the wrong way. I know he obviously hasn't forgotten how to get to Orville's. "Feel like taking the scenic route?"

Alec laughs along with me but doesn't answer.

I don't know what to think, but I don't feel like grilling him with all the questions that are in my head, so we sit comfortably in silence. When he wants me to know what's going on, he'll tell me. Until then, I'm okay with waiting. I trust him.

As Alec drives us forward, I realize we're heading east out of Syracuse, in the opposite direction of the Falls. My curiosity is definitely heightened now. I look over at my beautiful boyfriend. He smiles at me again, his eyes shining.

Yep.

He has something planned.

I know this for sure when we stop at a really good local "fast food" (but not really) burger place to take lunch with us on the drive.

We start chatting about work, a friend's party we went to last week, and the nothing at all kind of things that still lead to significant, treasured conversations. It's the kind of talk we had on our first date, when Ale wanted to know literally everything about me, even the things I considered dull or not worth discussing. Early afternoon becomes late afternoon, then early evening, and Alec and I are still traveling toward the east/southeast. Wherever we end up, it's a good thing I already have my overnight bag. Makes sense now why Alec didn't want me to spend a measly twenty extra seconds to put it in his apartment. I'm guessing he has a bag, too, most likely in his trunk. I'd placed mine in the back seat.

At some point, we stop for gas, snacks, and cold beverages, and also to stand and stretch our muscles. Being cooped up in a vehicle that long has me wishing we could wander around this tiny town in

Massachusetts for at least a little while, but—knowing Alec—we're on a schedule.

Most of those snacks are almost gone by the time I figure out that we must be heading to Boston, though I can't figure out why.

"Sox game?" I ask suddenly as the idea comes to me.

I'm actually thrilled at the thought of attending my first professional baseball game. Alec and I have gone to several different sporting events since we officially became a couple in February, but, as of yet, none of those have been professional leagues.

"You're pretty giddy at that idea." Alec smiles, clearly happy from my reaction. "But no."

Now I laugh. "Where are you taking me, boyfriend of mine?"

"I have a surprise planned for this weekend."

"Babe, it's Saturday night. Weekend's practically over." I laugh again.

Alec reaches over to squeeze my hand for a few seconds. "Do you really want to know?"

I think about this. Would knowing the surprise ahead of time ruin my excitement of it? Probably not, but maybe. I quickly shake my head. "Nope. I'm good with waiting."

"Love you, sweetness," Alec tells me with an affectionate look in his eyes. This is what he does when he's feeling a bit emotional but doesn't want to talk about it or let any of it out more than letting me know how he feels about me. Makes my heart flutter and my body dissolve to goo every time, especially when he calls me sweetness. He started doing that early in our relationship in celebration of the fact that I admitted to him—and pretty much only to him, besides my boss and friend Lourdes—that sweet peas are one of my favorite flowers.

At least twice a week, I find bouquets and vases of them on my desk or in my apartment, courtesy of my thoughtful boyfriend.

"I love you, too," I reply, knowing full well he put this heat into my cheeks and not the warm night air coming through my open window. Happens every time, even though we've been together for over six months now. He still gives me the same weak in the knees feeling I had when he first walked into Blooming Cascade Floral Design and left there with me on our first date.

Admittedly, the in-between of our first date and the official start of our relationship was rocky at best, aside from three glorious days snowed in with each other in my apartment, but those challenges helped solidify for us that we deserved to be together, fears or no fears.

Our drive into Cambridge, Massachusetts is riddled with traffic and a few road construction detours. Alec seems prepared, though, and we don't sit in any spot of traffic too long. Most likely, he researched all of this and checked it at least a dozen times this morning to be sure. I don't know where to assume we'll end up. Dinner? Hotel? Why would we come all the way out to Massachusetts?

Then we pull up to a large, imposing yet unassuming gray building.

Wait.

Science museum?

"Isn't the museum closed?" I ask, confused. "It's after-hours by now."

Except the parking lot isn't exactly empty. In fact, quite a few vehicles take up the spaces.

"How would you like appetizers, drinks, and an immersive experience?" He—of course—makes it sound as flirty as possible, the way he does with nearly everything he says to me. Alec's spoken to me like that pretty much since we met, most of the time not even realizing it. It's obvious to me when he speaks in his normal tone, and I hate it. I love him and his voice, but it's too jarring for him to not use the flirty tone.

"What kind of immersive experience?" I ask in return, my voice as flirty as my boyfriend's.

Since the car is already in park and turned off, Alec unbuckles, leans over, and hovers with his mouth nearly but not quite on mine. "Virtual, augmented, and mixed reality to start with." He lowers his voice, his eyes on my lips. His hands are on my thighs, his skin caressing mine below the edge of my shorts. "Then we can go back to the hotel and have any kind of experience you want."

"Do we have to hurry in here so we can go check into the hotel?" I ask, my voice breathy and soft. I move my gaze from his eyes to his mouth and back. I glance down again just in time to catch him slowly skimming his tongue over his bottom lip before moving his eyes up to meet mine. We both grin, then Alec leans back.

"I completed the mobile check-in while we were still at the gas station."

"So, no rush?"

He shakes his head. "Take all the time you want to enjoy this. Just so long as you're done before they close and kick us out."

I can't help but giggle.

In the museum, Alec and I wander through room after room of computerized "adventures," each as amazing as the last. There are games, nature tours, flying lessons—both piloted airplane and flying human—and so much more. Each requires different variations of headsets with built-in microphones and headphones, plus movement sensors, handheld controllers or joysticks, and powerful computers nearby that run everything. Some interactive experiences are demos, while others are fully functional games or apps.

After finishing up with the outer space one—which is seriously amazing—we take a break and wander over to the bar running the entire length of the far wall in the "main" event room. Though amazed at all our choices, we finally decide to snack on a few bacon-stuffed mushrooms and fig and goat cheese crostini. I don't know about him, but I'm a little too full from all the car snacks. Should have listened when he told me not to eat too many, but I didn't know at the time we'd have such an incredible array of delectable treats to choose from.

We finish our selected appetizers and move on to the next room.

"What's this one?" I ask as Alec eventually hands me a VR headset and a controller. There are multiple choices in this room for two-person teams, but he apparently wants this one the most. We've had to wait fifteen minutes for it. Once I put on the headset, the interactive game slash experience loads. We choose our avatars, then I smile as the experience starts. "Snow, huh?"

"It did bring us together," Alec says, a sweet warmth in his voice.

I wish I could see his eyes right now to soak in more of his love. The best I can do is lift my headset just enough to see the grin that's spreading on his handsome face.

A little reluctantly, I replace my headset again.

This isn't just snow. It's a snowball fight. Though Alec and I are the only real-life humans playing, both of us are fully equipped with a large grouping of virtual teammates and plenty of the faux fluffy white stuff for armor.

As we hurl computerized balls of snow at each other, I laugh. "Maybe we should have done this when we were trapped in my apartment."

A deep, rumbling chuckle comes from Alec's direction, followed by a soft growl. "Do you really wish we'd done that instead?"

I hold in a moan as the memories of what we did while snowed in come rushing to the forefront of my mind. "Not even a little bit." But the mood is too heady and serious between us now. I mean, we're surrounded by a room full of strangers. Not the time to let ourselves get turned on. We have the whole rest of the night for that, which is why I virtually scoop up the largest snowball I've made yet and throw it right in the face of the "Alec" avatar.

He laughs, of course, then drops down to his knees to scoop up as much "snow" as possible. But though he has amassed a giant snowball, he doesn't stand back up. Then I realize he isn't on his knees. He's on *one* knee.

My breath begins to quicken. I instinctively put a hand up to my sternum.

Alec holds out a snowball to me, but that can't be right.

I remove my headset, and am back to reality in enough time to see him remove his, too. He hands off the headset and controller to a man who stands nearby. Alec had talked to this man a little earlier while I was admiring the graphics showing on a screen several feet away. The museum logo and name tag on the man's shirt catch my eye.

The man steps closer to me, gently taking my headset and controller as well before disappearing into the crowd. Well, I think he does, but right now, I only have eyes for Alec, who's holding something in his hand that I hadn't noticed before now.

It takes several moments of blinking before I know for sure that I'm seeing what I think I am.

There in his right hand is a small, cream-colored box, which he then slowly opens to reveal a ring. Not just any ring. It's the gold engagement ring with the pear-shaped emerald I've sighed over for the past two months.

This shouldn't come as a shock. Honestly, it really doesn't. Alec and I have discussed marriage and our future together many times. But it's also the most wonderful surprise. I'm blinking rapidly again, only this time, it's to hold in the tears currently filling my eyes.

"Marce," Alec begins. Almost as soon as he starts speaking, he stops and clears his throat. "Marce, we haven't been dating very long. Less than a year."

I feel myself take a step closer to him as our gazes are locked on each other.

Alec continues. "In that time, I have loved every version of you. Whether it's Happy Marcy, Tired Marcy, Hangry Marcy, Scared Marcy, or so many others, I adore them all. I adore *you*."

We both sniffle, and I take another step closer, near enough to reach out if I could move anything on me beyond my feet. My right hand is still pressed to my sternum, the tips of my fingers splayed just below my left collarbone.

"Some might laugh at the way we got together. Some might shake their heads. None of that matters. Things might have been a little bumpy in the beginning, but I know you and I are meant to be together. I knew it way before I thought I was ready to tell you." He stops here to clear his throat again.

It's so quiet in this room, I assume everyone either left or is silently watching us. I don't care to look. I'm waiting for the moment when one specific, tiny, simple word can flow over my lips. When that tiny word, that eager answer to his beautiful question, helps propel us into a future I wasn't entirely sure I was ready to even dream of six months ago.

All the blinking I've done has been no use at all. My tears freely fall as I stay enraptured by this amazing man that I adore.

"I am so in love with you, Marcy," Alec says, reaching out to me. I move my right hand down to embrace his left one. "I once told you that we needed things to look forward to."

At this, I nod, vividly remembering that conversation from our first date.

A smile broadens across his face. He gives my hand a squeeze. "Will you marry me?"

I'm nodding again, as quickly as I can, my head bobbing over and over until I can tearfully find enough voice to say *the* word. "Yes!" I finally whisper-shout.

Alec moves like he's about to stand, but I can't wait another second without being in his arms. I practically lunge at him, nearly tackling him, surrounded by a chorus of cheers and whistles. I guess the other people in the room hadn't cleared out after all. My fiancé—fiancé!—wraps his arms around me and deftly pulls us both to our feet, since I now see we are precariously close to collapsing onto the floor.

We hold each other for several long moments, whispering I love yous, then pull back enough for Alec to be able to gently slide this wonderful symbol of forever onto my left ring finger.

"I am never taking this off," I say, sweeping my gaze back and forth between Alec's gorgeous emerald eyes and my gorgeous emerald ring.

He gives a little laugh. "Doesn't matter if you wear it every day or not at all, sweetness. I know the future we're going to have together."

I lightly tug him toward me, positioning my mouth close to his ear. My next words are for his listening pleasure only. "Does our immediate future still include any kind of experience I want at the hotel?"

Alec doesn't reply. He doesn't need to. I can tell by the glowing, wolfish expression on his face exactly what he's thinking. With the energy of a shooting star, he grips onto my hand and carefully pulls me out of the room, thanking all our well-wishers on the way. Before long, we are already in his car, driving over to the hotel. Neither of us even care that we skipped the last three exhibits.

Since we're already checked in, Alec grabs my bag from the back seat and his from the trunk, then leads me to our upper-floor room . . . I mean *suite*.

"Wow, babe," I whisper after we've stepped inside and turned on the lights, the door already closed behind us. I wasn't quite sure what to expect, but I truly believe this is even better than I could have imagined. To our left is a little hallway that leads to a slate gray and ice blue bathroom. Ahead, I see living and dining areas, as well as two doors. I assume one leads to a closet, the other to the bedroom. Everything is sleek and modern, light and also a little bold.

"Nice, huh?" Alec asks.

I turn to see that his eyes are on me, not the room.

"There's a library downstairs, too," he adds.

"Now you're just spoiling me."

He laughs, his face crinkling into a smile.

Moving toward him, I release the bags from his grip, lowering them to the hardwood floor beneath our feet. Almost immediately, Alec eliminates the space between us and takes my hands in his. Slowly and softly, he kisses both my hands, pausing with my left one up by his mouth. He drops his gaze to my ring. What he sees puts a rosy glow on his cheeks.

"How long have you been planning this?" I start to ask, but my words end up mumbled as Alec dips his head down to my neck.

My skin tingles before he even touches me. I involuntarily shudder with desire and attempt to wiggle closer, though our bodies are already pressed together from chest to toes. We release our hands at the same time, his soon resting on my hips. I slide mine from his waist up to his thick biceps then on and around his neck, spreading my fingers into his hair. This elicits a whispered moan—a rumble vibrating from his chest into mine as he caresses the skin of my neck with his lips.

We lose ourselves to this moment in time. There is an imperfect past behind us and a long, happy future ahead of us. The when, where, how, and with whom for the wedding will come at some point. Here, in this swanky hotel suite, the only thing that matters is now. He is my fiancé now, and I am his. We are together now, eagerly pulling at each other's clothes and kissing like the other holds the key to the only oxygen in the world. We are celebrating the future of us, *right now.*

·♥·♥·♥·♥·♥·

As we lie on our sides, our bodies mere inches from each other and our free arms draped over one another, our breathing synchronized, I tell myself once again that I'm the luckiest woman in the world. A soft glow of morning sunlight has already begun peeking around the edges of the closed window coverings, reminding us that we've been awake for most of the night.

"Since before we were officially together," Alec whispers, the tips of our noses barely touching. They're still close enough for me to feel the sensation of this.

"Since what?" I ask, sleepy and thoroughly sated, not just from the delicious room service food we ordered last night when we needed a breather. Well, when we reluctantly decided we should take a breather or risk missing out on dinner because room service was about to switch to their narrowed, late-night menu that didn't include the lobster mac and cheese Alec knew I'd love. Of course, he was right. He was probably also right when he suggested that a nap at some point would be a good idea, but I have zero regrets about not listening to him. Neither of us had *any* issues with keeping our stamina.

"The first time the thought occurred to me that you could be my bride." His voice is still muted.

"Oh," I reply, my voice as tender as his. "You never told me that before."

Alec chuckles. "I've made a fool of myself enough in front of you."

"We've both done that." I laugh along with him then lean in just enough to graze my lips against his in a sultry tease. I manage to pull back before he can hold me there, but he carefully tugs me toward him again and fully captures my mouth with his anyway. He squeezes my hip and I feel him smile through the kiss, both of us knowing he did exactly what I wanted him to do.

Innumerable seconds pass before Alec is finally able to speak again, his lips and mine blissfully swollen from our recent activity. "So, future wife." Here he pauses, allowing us both to luxuriate in this phrase. "How do you feel about brunch?"

"I don't know, future husband of mine," I say deliberately with a warm grin, giddy yet already comfortable with that word. *Husband*. Electrifying goose bumps prickle my skin at the very thought of it. "Will I get to sit with you?"

He places a brief kiss on the tip of my nose. "You won't get to sit *on* me." Then his eyes immediately darken at the intoxicating memories of what we did last night and earlier this morning on the floor, the sofa, and the incredibly fluffy, king size bed. I lean closer and plant a small kiss on his cheek before he continues. "But yes, you get to be with me, and I get to be with you."

Alec has already slipped his hands up to cup my cheeks, keeping my focus on his eyes. "Forever, Marce. You and me? That's forever."

I match his firm yet hushed tone. "There is no one I'd rather share forever with."

We share a soft kiss on the lips, then Alec pulls back. "Do you promise to never call me Dipshit Alec?"

"Of course." I struggle to hold in the giggle that wants to burst out of me. "I mean, it's all about the alliteration anyway, so really, you'd be Asshole Alec."

The slight twitch of his mouth is the only sign I have that Alec is also hiding how entertained he is. "Asshole Alec?"

Now I can't hold in a chuckle any longer. I set it free with a wide grin. My fiancé unleashes his amusement as well.

"That is the one and only time that phrase will be uttered," I tell him, grasping onto his arms and pulling us nearer to each other once again. Alec gives me what I silently ask for, wrapping both arms around my midsection, resting his forehead against mine, our bare skin in contact from head to nearly toe. "I absolutely promise," I add.

"I promise you this, too, Marce. We might find a lot of fitting alliterations for each other, but my words for you will only ever mean one thing. My love. My wife. My Marcy."

# Extra Bonus Epilogue

## Marcy

"Brats and hot dogs on now. Burgers will be on soon. All of it should be done in about fifteen, maybe twenty minutes," Pete tells Alec and me as we go to check on the grill.

"You don't have to do this," Alec says yet again. He tried his best to insist on cooking the food and not allowing our guests to do any work. Pete responded by telling Alec that he's not just a guest, he's his best friend, and Alec shouldn't have to worry about anything on his birthday.

His thirty-fifth, to be exact. My husband loves celebrating his birthday, so of course I wanted to throw him a party to mark this milestone. The middle of his thirties, which I'll reach soon enough myself. I also have a special surprise for him. But that's not until later. Right now, I'm getting the salads and side dishes out onto the food table, along with plates, utensils, and napkins. There's a cake in the fridge waiting for later, as well as fresh fruit and veggie trays our guests have been welcome to snack on all day.

When I step into the kitchen again, double checking that I'm not missing anything and noticing I haven't gotten the buns out yet, Alec steps behind me. "I've got some buns you'll like," he whispers.

I laugh, hoping he made sure to check no one was around when he said it. "You definitely do, but that'll have to wait. Not sure our guests would appreciate you taking those buns out right now."

"We could make them all go home," he says as he nuzzles into my neck.

"Sorry to interrupt, but are the burgers in here?" Pete says. We turn to find him standing near the doorway. "Thought I brought them out with me, but there's only sausage in that dish."

Since I know exactly what my husband would say to me if we were alone, I laugh. Alec and Pete both smirk, I assume because they both know, too. "Yeah. Let me get them for you."

I remove the foil-covered platter of burger patties from the refrigerator and hand it to Pete as well as a few packages of brat and burger buns. "Thanks, Pete."

He nods with a smile, then heads back outside.

"So, what were we talking about?" Alec asks, stepping toward me, his eyes on my lips. "Buns and sausages, right?"

A brown blur runs past us, panting, nails clicking on the tile, through the kitchen out onto the patio, easily maneuvering through the magnetic screen door, even with the leash still attached to his harness.

Blazer. My surprise birthday present for Alec, just a little early. I hadn't expected my friend Cass here so soon. She barrels into the room calling the dog's name as Alec and I immediately step to the patio, hoping to catch him. Cass joins us outside as she and I call him now. But Blazer's too happy meeting new people and sniffing new things to bother listening.

"Hey," I say, as I turn and look at Cass, knowing Blazer's okay for the moment now that he's away from the grill and getting attention from Lourdes and Spence, who are both scratching behind Blazer's ears. "Hadn't expected you right now." I can't exactly say she's early since she's actually late to the party. Alec doesn't know this was planned.

"Yeah. I couldn't make it at the time you said. Sorry." She gives me an apologetic expression.

I smile in return. "It's okay. Glad you're here now. And Blazer, too," I add, only when I turn to glance at him, he's gone. I look around the yard, but he's nowhere to be found. He never ran past us, and the yard is fenced.

"Hey," I say after Cass and I walk over to Lourdes, who hands me the leash they kindly removed from Blazer's harness. No sense in him having to drag it around everywhere. I thank her, then ask, "Where did the dog go?"

"Some of the kids where throwing a foam football around over there." She points to a back corner of the yard. "He bounced over there, but I guess he isn't there anymore. Need help looking for him?"

Lourdes is the only other person who knows why Blazer is here. "Yes, please," I say to her.

The three of us spread out, but there are people in the front and back yards as well as in the house. Blazer could be anywhere. The kids tell me he walked away as soon as one of them threw a stray ball toward the left side of the yard. If he went that way, he easily could have made it back in the house without Cass and I noticing because of the rose bushes nearby.

I check the house, starting with the kitchen. To my dismay, the first thing I find is Cass picking up ripped pieces of wrapping paper. Blazer's work, I assume. He must have jumped up, considering he's tall enough to reach the top of the table with his front paws.

"I'm sorry," she says as soon as I squat down to help her. "He wasn't like this when he was staying with me. My cousin said he never made messes at the rescue."

"It's okay. Maybe he's never been around this much excitement before. We won't mind training him. Right now we just need to find him," I reassure her with a smile. Once the mess is cleaned up, and Alec's presents are safe on the once again, if not partially opened, I continue my search for the German shepherd. He has to be around here somewhere.

From where I stand, I can see out the front and back windows. Neither Lourdes nor Cass look like they see him anywhere. We do have a few doors open in the house, including bedrooms. Blazer could be in one of them. I walk up the stairs to check, just in case. Then I hear a familiar voice, and what sounds like the thumping of a long tail on the floor.

I enter our home office to find Alec sitting on the floor with Blazer, the dog's tail hitting the carpet as he wags in happiness while Alec pets the top of Blazer's head. "Hey," I say softly. "Guess you're the lucky one who found him."

"Yeah, I caught him grabbing one of the presents and followed him up here." Alec holds up a partially-wrapped thin box that looks like it might be some kind of board game.

"I'm sorry about the presents," I tell him, unsure how to inform him of the rest. "It feels like it's been nothing but chaos for the past half hour or so. But I'm glad you two are getting along so well."

Alec looks up at me and smiles as I join them on the floor. "He's pretty cool," he says.

"Would you still think that if I told you Blazer is actually your present from me?"

Now Alec looks up at me with a wide grin. "Seriously?"

I nod.

Alec shifts up on to his knees, leaning toward me before claiming my lips with his. We become a tangle of lips and tongues until the dog puts his cold, wet nose against Alec's arm, wanting attention. Before my sweet husband refocuses on him, he moves his gaze back to me.

"Thank you, honey. He's the perfect present, but still not as good as you are. I love you."

"Love you, too."

He scruffs up the fur behind Blazer's ears before petting his head again. "I'm happy we get to keep him. He's a little rambunctious, but I'm sure we can run him around the yard every day or take walks to the park. It'll be okay. Crunch will like him, too."

With a smile, I reply, "He already does. I've been slowly introducing them this past week when you've worked over or gone out with the guys."

"So, that's where you've been going with him. Well, I'm glad our little family is growing, Marce. We'll have Crunch and Blazer." His eyes start to light up. "Maybe we can get a rabbit, too. I had one when I was little. A rabbit and a duck. Maybe another cat."

"Are we going to end up with our own little menagerie?" I ask with a laugh. "One of every kind of pet?"

"If we do, I'll still love you more. I love you always, My Marcy."

"I love you, too, Alec. So much so that I'll even live in a zoo for you if that'll make you happy."

He smirks, like he's trying really hard to hold in a laugh. "The Russells' Petting Zoo. We can have goats, sheep, maybe a miniature horse or cow. Some chickens, though they wouldn't appreciate being touched. That's our future, Marcy Russell." Then he winks.

I wink back. Zoo or not, we have a wonderful future ahead of us, and I'm so ready for it.

"I'll Never Not Love You" | Michael Buble
  "I Think I Fell In Love Today" | Kelsea Ballerini
  "ceilings" | Lizzie McAlpine
  "Let It Snow" | Gwen Stefani
  "Everytime" | Britney Spears
  "Have A Little Faith In Me" | John Hiatt
  "Just You" | Amy Stroup
  "love is just a word" | Jasmine Thompson, Calum Scott
  "Falling Like The Stars" | James Arthur
  "Take Me Out To The Ballgame" | Champs United
  "Centerfield" | John Fogerty
  "Everything Has Changed (feat. Ed Sheeran) (Taylor's Version)"
| Taylor Swift, Ed Sheeran
  "Feelings Show" | Colbie Caillat
  "Make You Feel My Love" | Adele
  "Thing of Beauty" | Danger Twins

# *Want more Lost Hearts Found?*

LOOK FOR **THROWAWAY RULES,** book 3 of Lost Hearts Found, and read all about how Lourdes and Spence fake date their way to a second chance at love.

Sign up for my newsletter for fun updates on my books, free goodies, and more! Subscribe at https://lisakeiferauthor.com/

If you enjoyed this book, please consider leaving a review. If you peruse reviews to see what readers liked about a novel, you might understand how important this can be. And thank you! As an indie author, I sincerely appreciate it.

*Also by Lisa Keifer*

## Lost Hearts Found:

Accidental Pasts
June Days
Winter Blossoms
Throwaway Rules
Uncharted Avenues
Holiday Distractions

www.ingramcontent.com/pod-product-compliance
Lightning Source LLC
Chambersburg PA
CBHW061546310726

48972CB00008B/2630